69 Barrow Street

LAWRENCE BLOCK
writing as Sheldon Lord

CLASSIC EROTICA

---

21 Gay Street
Candy
Gigolo Johnny Wells
April North
Carla
A Strange Kind of Love
Campus Tramp
Community of Women
Born to be Bad
College for Sinners
Of Shame and Joy
A Woman Must Love
The Adulterers
Kept
The Twisted Ones
High School Sex Club
I Sell Love
69 Barrow Street
Four Lives at the Crossroads
Circle of Sinners
A Girl Called Honey
Sin Hellcat
So Willing

CLASSIC EROTICA #18

69 BARROW STREET

Lawrence Block

Chapter 1

Everything happens in Greenwich Village.

The Village extends from Fourteenth Street to Houston Street, from the East River to the Hudson. The buildings are low for New York, with a seven-story structure a rarity. Once a young man who liked to pretend he was a poet described the Village as the valley between the breasts of Manhattan, with skyscrapers to the north and skyscrapers to the south.

Greenwich Village is many things to many people.

Long ago it was the headquarters of artists, writers, dancers and musicians. They were attracted to the spot because it was a sort of an oasis in the middle of the Manhattan jungle, complete with an informal, small-townish air about it, cheap restaurants and low rents.

That was long ago.

Times have changed. So has the Village.

The cheap restaurants are tourist traps now. High priced strip clubs dot Third Street, fighting for space with homosexual and lesbian hangouts. Rents have skyrocketed as the Village has become the fashionable place for people who want to feel artistic.

The artists are long gone, although the streets are still cluttered with phonies who sketch charcoal studies of tourists at two to five dollars a throw. The writers are long gone, although there are still the ones who live on unemployment and peck at typewriters, pretending to be writers but incapable of writing anything more complex than their own names. The musicians are gone and the dancers are gone.

Only the dregs remain.

The junkies, who punch holes in their arms with hypodermic needles and live in a world of cocaine and heroin and morphine, a sticky pink world of nothing happening, a world where the only important activity is taking a fix and the only important person is the connection, the pusher, the Man.

The queers, male and female. Fags, dykes, queens, swishes, homos, lesbos, butches. The gay set, a subculture with a thousand nicknames. Drifting back and forth in shadows, men with false breasts and lipstick on their mouths, women in pants who swagger and curse like truck drivers.

And the Sick Ones—not junkies or queers necessarily, but sick, twisted, perverted men and women out on a hell-for-leather hunt for kicks, for something new and something different.

The Sick Ones.

Ralph Lambert lived at 69 Barrow Street.

Barrow Street is a small, narrow, quiet street almost undistinguishable from a dozen other Village streets. It runs west from Sheridan Square toward the Hudson River for about a half dozen blocks of quiet brownstones with an occasional small restaurant or tavern. There is little traffic on Barrow Street during the day and hardly any at all at night.

Barrow Street is a quiet street, a pleasant street. The apartments in the four- or five-story brownstones rent for somewhat more than they are worth, but the apartments are clean and relatively modern.

Barrow Street could be a nice place to live.

Ralph Lambert hated it.

It wasn't the street that he hated, he reflected. Or if it was, it wasn't the street's fault. It wasn't even the apartment, although God knew if he had a chance he'd do it over. Stella's idea of interior decoration was pretty vile. If she liked a piece of furniture or a scatter-rug or a print she bought it, never caring how it went with the rest of the furnishings. And the result was pretty disorganized, with modern abstracts and colonial chairs and oriental rugs all in the same room.

He lit a cigarette, trying to be comfortable in the uncomfortable colonial chair and staring blankly into the fireplace. The fireplace was a fake, of course. If anyone should be stupid enough to start a fire in it he would probably burn the building down, since there was no chimney for it.

But a genuine fireplace would have been out of place, just as anything genuine wouldn't have belonged at 69 Barrow Street. Everything had to be fake and phony in order to fit in.

Just as the apartment was phony.

Just as Stella was phony. Stella James, the tigress with the biggest breasts and the longest, blondest hair in the world, and God what a bitch she was. And how he hated her.

He laughed bitterly. Hell, who was he to talk? Who was he to call anybody phony? For that matter, who was he to hate Stella? And if he hated her and the place so much, why in hell didn't he get out?

He flicked the ashes from his cigarette onto the floor. Hell, he *ought* to be able to get out. He was free, white, and over 21. 27, to be exact. And it wasn't as though he had to let Stella support him for the rest of his life. At the bottom he was a pretty talented guy. He was hardly another Rembrandt, but he could make a paintbrush behave and the stuff he turned out wasn't bad to look at. Not good enough so that he could paint what he wanted to paint, but decent enough to land him some sort of job in commercial art. A little work and a little effort and he could be making fifteen grand a year for life.

If he left Stella.

He laughed again to himself, this time more bitterly than the first time. *If he left Stella.* That was one hell of a big *if.* It was almost the same as saying if he had wings he could fly.

Well, why not? Why not grow wings and then fly away from 69 Barrow Street to someplace sane? Christ, he hadn't been like this all his life, lying around the apartment all day long and making love to a tigress all night. He had been a painter and a fairly good one. How had he let himself get so thoroughly screwed up?

Why, he hadn't so much as had a paintbrush in his hand for more than two months. And he hadn't really accomplished anything remotely decent in over a year, not since the one and only painting he did of Stella just after they started living together. And now where was he?

A gigolo. Oh, he didn't have to call himself that all the time. Most of the time he managed to lie to himself, telling himself and the world that he was an artist and couldn't take the time to work, couldn't prostitute his talent to make a living. But that was so much nonsense. He was a gigolo and that was all there was to it. Stella kept him, kept him like other women kept pet dogs or cats or monkeys. Instead of walking him on a leash she put him to work in a bedroom; instead of parading him around in Washington Square on Sunday afternoons she paraded him around the apartment twenty-four hours a day, seven days a week. She dominated him and she loved to dominate him.

And he took it. He sat back and took it because he didn't have the guts to do anything about it. He lay around the apartment living on the money Stella's father had left her and he never did a goddamned thing, nothing at all.

Why?

Why Stella, for God's sake? Hell, if he wanted to be kept he could do better than her. The Village was full of beautiful, frustrated women who wanted a good-looking guy as a plaything. Maybe most of them didn't have Stella's looks and weren't as imaginative or as competent as Stella in bed, but with them he wouldn't have to take what he took from her. Life with somebody else wouldn't be a constant routine of agony and humiliation, of torment and insults and hating himself.

And he could get damn near any woman he wanted. He knew he could; he had always been able to. Part of it was his rugged good looks—the jet black, curly hair, the broad shoulders and the slim waist, the strong muscles in his arms and legs. The strong chin, the full mouth, even the scar on one cheek where a sailor had caught him with a broken beer bottle years ago—all these features added up to the sort of appearance that had the women flat on their backs with their legs spread the minute he snapped his fingers.

So why in hell was he killing himself with a Grade A, first class, number one bitch on wheels like Stella James?

Why?

He flipped his cigarette into the phony fireplace and pulled another from the pack, placing it between his lips. He scratched a wooden match on the underside of the end-table and lit the cigarette, flipping the match into the fireplace. He drew deeply on the cigarette and held the smoke in his lungs for several seconds, expelling it finally in a long, thin stream that wandered slowly to the ceiling.

Hell, he knew why. He knew why he stayed with Stella, why he did what she told him and took the abuse she hurled at him constantly. Why he was able to stand it all, to stand the things that a normal man shouldn't be able to stand. Things like letting other men make love to her and forcing him to watch from the closet. As if he wasn't man enough for her!

She even took women as lovers and made him watch the two of them perform.

And he took it, all of it, the insults and the torture and all the rest. And he knew why.

Because he loved her.

He loved her and he hated her. He hated her for what she was but he couldn't help loving her for what she was at the same time. He needed her as he had never needed any woman before. All the things that he hated about her only made her more exciting, more desirable, more thrilling than any other woman he had ever met. And so he was tied to her by invisible threads, tied up so securely that he could never get away.

He dragged on the cigarette. It tasted terrible, and he wondered if it was the cigarette that tasted lousy or that he was smoking too much, or just the generally bad taste in his mouth that came when he spent too much time thinking about himself and Stella, about the sick, twisted life he was living and the sick, horrible, beautiful, wonderful, damnable woman he loved and hated and surrendered to: Stella.

Impulsively he hurled the cigarette into the fireplace and watched the sparks dance up into the air a few feet. Then he pulled himself up from the chair and stalked to the window, scanning the area outside.

Barrow Street.

Ralph Lambert hated Barrow Street. He hated the men and women walking quietly by, the kids playing stoop ball a few houses away, the old Italian peddling ice cream on a stick from a wagon down the block, he hated everything about Barrow Street.

And he knew what it was that he really hated.

He hated Ralph Lambert.

Susan Rivers was afraid.

She had been afraid ever since early that morning, when she had passed the beautiful woman on the way to her new apartment. The beautiful woman was very blonde and very tall and very well built and very lovely, and Susan Rivers was very much afraid of her.

She had just moved into the apartment that morning. Before that she lived on Gay Street—which she thought was particularly appropriate—but then Gloria had decided to fall in love with another girl and she had to find a place for herself. So she had found this place on Barrow Street.

She located the apartment through an ad in the *Village Voice*, a neighborhood newspaper which combined excellent columns and reviews with news on everything going on in the area. The ad had said, simply:

> BARROW ST., lg. liv. rm., kitch.,
> bath, $85, apply supt., 69 Barrow.

Which meant, simply enough, that she had to apply to the superintendent at 69 Barrow Street for an $85-a-month apartment with a large living room, a kitchen, and a bath. That was Thursday, and she applied to the super that afternoon, signed the lease, packed her belongings and brought them from Gloria's apartment the next morning.

And met the beautiful woman on the steps.

Not because she met a woman, or even because the woman was beautiful. Susan was a lesbian, but that didn't mean that she wanted to hop into the hay with every good-looking gal she bumped into. Hardly. She had her own desires, and although her desires were classed as abnormal, they were not overwhelming compulsions which she couldn't overcome. She was a lesbian simply because she found women more attractive than men.

Well, it was more complex than that, she admitted. There was the fact that men scared her silly, that the mere thought of letting a man enter her and touch her inside had her shivering. And a psychiatrist could probably delve into her mind and figure out even more complex reasons for the way she was, but to hell with all psychiatrists. She was what she was, and she was damned if she was going to start worrying about it now.

But the woman worried her, worried her very much. For one thing, she couldn't remember being so strongly attracted to anyone before. More important, she could tell that the attraction was not all on her part.

They had met on the steps. Susan was carrying a suitcase and the woman stepped aside to let her pass. As she did so she could feel the woman's hot, insistent eyes burning into her slender body. She felt the woman's warm breath near her cheek.

And she knew that the woman wanted her.

It would be so easy, so easy to go off on another hot sex bout. Easy—and very nice. But God, after the thing with Gloria ended on the rocks she had been so damned determined to sleep alone for a while, to just relax and spend some time by herself until she got a clearer idea of who the hell she was and where the hell she was going. She had been so damned determined, and now look at her. Just another dyke with hot pants who couldn't look at another girl's breasts without wanting to kiss them, who couldn't pass close to another female body without itching to cover it with her own.

God!

Que sera sera. That was how that song went, and it made its own kind of sense. Whatever will be will be, whatever would happen would happen, and she would just let things happen to her. It would work out; everything always worked out.

But Christ how she wanted to see that woman again!

She heaved a sigh and sat down on the edge of her bed. It was a single bed, and that at least was a good sign. If she got in the mood for any horizontal acrobatics she could go someplace else instead of making love in her own apartment. In her own place she could be alone by herself.

She stood up and decided to take a nap for an hour or two. She undressed slowly, baring a body that was slim and tan and boyishly beautiful. Her breasts were small but perfect, and she was by no means flat-chested. Her dark brown hair was cut short and her legs tapered from full, rounded thighs to trim ankles.

It was a nice body. She wondered how the blonde woman would like it.

When she was completely nude and ready for bed she threw back the covers and stretched out on the clean white sheet. She rested her head on the pillow and let her eyes close.

In her mind she pictured the blonde woman. Thinking about her, she let her own hands caress her body. She cupped her breasts, feeling the softness and firmness of them and imagining in her mind that it was the other woman's breasts she was holding and that the woman was embracing her. Then she moved her hands down to the lean, flat stomach and stroked gently, rhythmically.

Everything was so quiet, so peaceful and so gentle. She relaxed completely and continued to stroke herself, her hands lingering on the inside of her thighs where the skin was so extraordinarily soft and tender. She remembered the way Gloria had loved to touch and kiss her there, and in her mind she saw the blonde woman doing the same.

Then her hands moved to the spot where no man had ever been and she stroked herself gently, languorously, feeling warm sensations of love course through her young body. Deliciously obscene pictures flooded her mind as she handled herself until she drifted off into a deep, heady, luxurious sleep.

It was almost 5:30 in the afternoon when Stella James mounted the steps at 69 Barrow Street and fitted her key in the lock. Anticipation coursed through her as she walked to the door of the apartment she shared with Ralph.

She was hungry.

She giggled to herself as she thought of the word. *Hungry.* That was what Frank had called her years ago. He said she was the hungriest woman he had ever met, and he was probably right.

"Don't you ever get enough?" he had demanded.

"Never," she said. "When I've had enough it'll be time for them to bury me."

Frank had been the first, and there had been so many after him that she had lost count. She couldn't even recall what some of them looked like or what their names were. Old men, young men, boys even—she thought fleetingly of a delivery boy, just a freshman in high school, who couldn't have been more than fourteen or fifteen. What a sweet, funny, excited little thing he had been! He brought her an order from the grocery once—God, it had been two or three years ago!—and she came to the door in a kimono.

From there on it had been easy. She let the kimono slip open persistently and each time she took longer to close it again. The poor kid, he couldn't help staring at her. And then she took him by the hand and led him inside and helped him off with his clothes. And she lay down beside him on her bed and showed him what to do . . .

Old men, young men and boys. And girls as well, of course. Sex was such a spectacularly wonderful thing that there was no point in drawing the line anywhere. It was as nice one way as the other.

She hesitated at her door, remembering the girl she had passed on the steps that morning. The girl was gay; there was no doubt about it. And the girl was interested in a roll in the hay as well. There was no doubt about that either.

Stella was interested herself. It had been almost a month since she had had a girl and she wanted one, wanted this one in particular. And it would be damned convenient having her living in the same building.

Almost reluctantly she turned her key in the door and stepped inside. There would be plenty of time for the girl later. Right now she wanted Ralph. She wanted to make him grovel at her feet and then have him possess her, harshly, violently.

She alternately liked and despised Ralph. All in all she thought him a pretty despicable individual, weak and spineless and totally dependent on her. Not many men would be willing or able to take what she dished out.

But at the same time he was a marvelous lover, and easily as virile a man as she had ever met. And he had an incredible imagination.

Besides, she needed a man like Ralph, a man she could push around whatever way she felt like. In his own way he loved her, and in her own way she supposed she loved him. Hardly the storybook kind of love with a picket fence and children, but love just the same. They were in the same boat.

He was sitting on the couch in the living room. When she walked in he looked up at her but said nothing. She smiled.

"Well?"

"What do you want me to say?"

Her smile widened. "You might tell me how nice I look."

He shrugged. "You look fine."

She did, and she knew it. She was wearing a lemon-colored sack dress just a shade deeper than her hair, and she had the sort of figure that kept a sack dress from looking like a sack. Her breasts and hips rubbed against the yellow material as she walked and accentuated all the sensuous lines of her full body.

"You look fine," he repeated. "Is that all you want?"

"Do you think it is?"

He shrugged again, feigning boredom.

"I want to talk to you," she said. "Why else would I come in here? I just want to have a nice, pleasant conversation with my lover."

He just looked at her.

She sat down next to him and slipped one arm around him so that her breast pressed into his shoulder. He tried to ignore her but she could sense how she was exciting him, how he wanted her. This was going to be good.

"I met a girl today," she said. "She just moved into this building."

"Oh?"

"She's very pretty," she went on. "Young, small—a lesbian, of course."

He laughed. "You make it sound as though every girl in the Village is a lesbian."

"Most of them are."

"And I suppose you intend to have her?"

"Of course."

"Suppose she doesn't want to be had?"

"She'll want to," Stella said. "I can tell."

"Stella," he demanded, "what in hell is the matter with you? Do you have to crawl in bed with everyone you see?"

"Only with my friends."

"And you don't have any enemies."

"That's right," she said, smiling.

He turned away from her. "Leave me alone."

"Don't be silly."

"Well, what the hell do you want from me?"

"I told you. I want to talk about the girl."

He sighed.

"She's very pretty, as I said. I think you'll like her."

"What the hell's the difference whether or not *I* like her?"

"Well," she said, "you're going to watch, of course. You might as well like what you're looking at."

"You bitch."

She pouted. "That's not nice, Ralph. You always watch. You know that."

He didn't say anything.

"You don't have to," she said. "You can always get out and leave and take your paints and brushes with you. Of course you'd starve to death, but—"

"Shut up!"

She laughed, delighted. She let one hand drop to his thigh and squeezed him, gently. "Or else you can watch. Maybe we can make it more exciting for you this time, dear. Maybe you can have the girl when I'm done with her."

Ralph looked at her, puzzled. "But she won't want that, will she? If she's a lesbian—"

"She might not have any choice in the matter, dear. I could help you, if you think it's too much for you."

He stared at her, his eyes wide with shock. "You don't mean–"

"That's exactly what I mean."

"God! Stella, don't you have any feeling for people? Don't you—"

"Oh, shut up," she commanded. Suddenly she was bored with the game. It was amusing the way Ralph was so easily shocked, as if he wasn't as depraved as she herself was. But she didn't feel in the mood for conversation any longer.

"Stand up," she ordered.

He stood up.

"Now take off your clothes."

He moved to the window to shut it but she stopped him. "Leave it open," she said. "So what if somebody watches? I don't care."

He started to protest, then stopped and began to remove his clothing. She stood motionless before him until he was completely nude. There was a mocking smile on her face.

She stepped closer to him until mere inches separated them. Then suddenly she clenched her left hand into a fist and drove it into his solar plexus. When he doubled up in agony her open right hand lashed out and caught him across the face. Her fingers left long red marks where they struck him.

He didn't say anything.

She smiled. "That's for arguing with me," she said. "That was your punishment. Now you can have your reward."

She reached down and lifted the sack dress to her waist. There was nothing under the dress.

"I think I'll leave the dress on," she said. "It's fun that way sometimes."

He still said nothing. He was numb with anger and desire in equal parts, wanting to love her and possess her and kill her. And so he remained silent and motionless.

She stretched out on her back on the oriental rug, her dress up around her waist. She looked up at him, a smile playing with the corners of her mouth.

"Come on," she said. "What are you waiting for?"

He took her, furiously and brutally and savagely, and all the while her cruel discordant laughter rang in his ears.

CHAPTER 2

Morning.

Ralph Lambert rolled out of the bed gingerly, being careful not to wake Stella. He yawned and rubbed sleep from his eyes. Then, before leaving the bedroom, he stood silently by the side of the bed and looked down at Stella.

She was sound asleep, her mouth pressed against the side of the pillow and her lush white body curled like a cat about to spring. Sleep softened the hard lines around her mouth and eyes and made her far more gentle and feminine than she was when she was awake. She invariably slept nude, and because the night was so warm she had thrown back the covers and slept on top of the bed.

Ralph saw her with the eye of an artist. While any man would have been captivated and excited by Stella's body, Ralph was able to study it in detail and to realize just how beautiful it was.

Stella was thirty, three years older than Ralph. With the sort of life she had been leading it was almost a miracle that no signs of wear or aging appeared to the eye. Her breasts were still perfectly firm, and breasts as large as Stella's generally show the signs of age earlier than smaller ones. Her complexion was clear and perfect from head to toe.

She was so beautiful, Ralph mused. How could anyone so beautiful be so inexplicably bad? It was impossible to understand.

He left the bedroom and closed the door behind him. A fast shower made him feel alive once again, his skin fresh and clean and his mind able to concentrate. He toweled himself dry and stood at the open bathroom window, gulping huge breaths of the early morning air. The air was as fresh as air ever got in New York and it made him feel even more awake and more alive.

He almost felt good.

But not quite. Not quite, because he knew that no man in his position could ever feel good. No man with Stella hanging on his neck like a millstone.

A millstone? That wasn't a particularly good image, and he closed his eyes to hunt for a better one. An albatross, perhaps. A sexy blonde albatross. He remembered the poem by Coleridge in which a sailor shot an albatross and the corpse of the bird hung around his neck for months bringing terrible luck to the ship.

That was Stella, all right. Hanging around his neck and lousing him up.

Returning to the bedroom, he dressed quickly and quietly. Stella slept on. He glanced at her again and the events of the previous night flashed through his mind briefly—the insults, the slapping, the humiliating way she had forced him to make love to her on the floor with her dress on, the terrible laughter that tore from her throat all the while until passion caught her up and the laughter changed in midstream to a gush of foul obscenities. For a moment a wild impulse gripped him and he longed to kill her, to press the pillow over her nose and mouth and hold it there until she choked to death.

But the impulse passed quickly. Ralph was not by nature a violent man. He could fight when pressed and he could lose his temper easily enough, but he had never yet gotten mad enough to commit murder.

But he had to admit the idea was an attractive one.

For a moment he considered frying himself a couple eggs in the apartment's small kitchen. Then he decided against it. He didn't want to be around when Stella woke up. Even if he didn't get up the guts to leave her, he wanted to spend as little time around her and the apartment as possible.

He left the apartment and walked down the hallway to the door. The weather was nice out, with a hot yellow sun just coming into view and the sky clear blue with hardly a cloud in it. He sat down for a moment on the stoop in front of the building and lit the first cigarette of the day, enjoying the lift it gave him as the strong smoke hit his lungs.

When the door opened behind him a second or two later he turned his head slightly to see who it was. That's when he saw her for the first time.

She was wearing black toreador pants that were tight around her hips and legs and a light green sleeveless blouse that looked as cool as the grass in the mountains. She wore sandals on her feet and her hair was short and dark brown. Her body was trim and neat; in fact, there was an overwhelming impression of neatness and coolness and quiet self-possession about her which hit him at once.

He liked her instantly.

"Hello," he said. He smiled.

She smiled back.

"I haven't seen you around before," he said. "Did you just move in recently?"

"Yesterday morning."

"First time in New York?"

"No," she said, and she smiled as if the question were very funny.

"Been in the Village before?"

She nodded. "For several years."

Suddenly he said, "Sit down for a minute. It's very nice here."

She seemed to be hesitating.

"Come on," he said, indicating that she could sit on the stoop beside him. "The sun's nice and it's still cool out. Later in the day you'll want to spend your time sitting in front of a fan, but now it's nice enough just sitting in the sun and enjoying it."

"All right," she said. "But only for a minute." She sat down.

He wasn't sure where to begin. He felt that he wanted to get to know this girl, wanted to talk to her, but it was hard to hit on a conversational opener. Still, she was obviously willing to talk with him. Otherwise she wouldn't have sat down.

"My name's Ralph," he said. "Ralph Lambert."

"I'm Susan Rivers."

"Have you had breakfast, Susan?"

"Not yet. I just got up."

"There's a place down the street where they make a good mushroom omelet. Interested?"

She hesitated, and this time it wasn't hard to see her hesitation.

She seemed genuinely worried about something and he wondered idly what it might be.

"I'm not trying to make a pass," he assured her. "I live on the first floor here and there's a girl who lives with me, so I'm not a guy on the make. I just thought you might like to have breakfast with me."

She relaxed visibly. "All right," she said. "A mushroom omelet sounds like a good idea."

They stood up simultaneously and began walking along Barrow Street toward the restaurant, a small quiet place around the corner on Bedford. He noticed things: the way the top of her head was just level with his shoulder, the clean freshly bathed smell of her that rose to his nostrils, the cool, calm air about her. As they walked they talked about nothing in particular and he hardly managed to follow the conversation even though he was a participant in it. His mind was wrapped up in an appraisal of the girl. He felt that he wanted to get to know her, wanted to find out for himself just what sort of a person she was and what made her tick.

They both ordered mushroom omelets at the restaurant, with orange juice and toast and coffee. They ate in relative silence— the food was good and they were both quite hungry.

Then, over coffee and cigarettes he said, "Do you work, Susan?"

She nodded.

"Where?"

"Do you know the ceramic and jewelry shop on Macdougal Street just below Eighth?"

"I think so."

"That's where I work. I design ceramics and do a little of the actual throwing myself, too."

"That sounds pretty good."

She shrugged. "It doesn't pay much but I like it. I can work pretty much my own hours and knock off for a day or two whenever I feel like it. And it's . . . well, creative, I guess."

"That makes a difference."

"It really does, Ralph. I'm not talking about the artistic angle of it or anything. I don't pretend to be artistic, whatever that means exactly. I'm just making things—ashtrays and vases and bowls that people can use and enjoy. It's more a craft than an art.

"But the thing is that I'm figuring out a way to make something and then making it, sort of with my own two hands." She held up her hands to illustrate the point. He noted that her hands were quite small with slender and well-formed fingers. Her fingernails were clipped short and she didn't wear any nail polish.

He said, "I know what you mean."

"It's a feeling of building something," she went on. "It makes a difference, a tremendous difference. Sometimes I get the feeling that my life is just a waste, that I'm not doing anything important and I might as well not be alive at all. But then I put on a smock and go in the workroom behind the shop and put some clay on the wheel and throw a pot and bake it and glaze it and . . . it just makes me feel a lot better, Ralph. As if I've accomplished something. As if I have a . . . a reason for existing, if you can understand what I'm trying to say."

"I understand."

They fell silent. He took a last drag on his cigarette and ground it out in the glass ashtray on the table. He felt very comfortable with her, more comfortable than he had felt with a woman in years. There was a definite feeling of ease between them, as if they understood and appreciated and respected each other, thinking the same things and experiencing the same emotions. Why, her attitude about her ceramics work was damned similar to his own feelings about his painting.

As if she were reading his mind she asked, "What do you do, Ralph?"

"Not much of anything."

She waited for him to explain.

"I'm a painter," he said at length. "Or at least I *was* a painter. I haven't done anything in months."

"How come?"

"I don't know. I've been in an awful slump, Susan. I just haven't had the slightest desire to do any work. My brushes don't even feel right in my hand anymore. Not too long ago I set up the easel in my front room and hauled out the paints and brushes. And I stood there looking at the canvas and I didn't know what to do or where to begin. I felt like a damned fool, just standing there pretending to be an artist and not even getting a drop of paint on the canvas."

"That's awful."

"It's a weird sort of feeling. Guys I've talked to say it can happen in any line of work. There's even a term for it—a writer friend of mine calls it *writer's block.* He says it happens to him every once in a while and there's not a damn thing he can do about it."

"I guess you just have to ride it out, huh?"

"I don't know," he said. "In my case I think it's something

different. It's not just that I can't paint, it's that I don't even want to paint anymore."

"You'll probably snap out of it."

"I guess so."

"You will, Ralph. All you have to do is keep trying. I think you'll make it."

He smiled at her.

Stella woke up like a cat. First her eyes opened slowly and closed again. Then she opened her eyes a second time and stretched herself slightly, tensing the muscles in her legs and reaching up over her head with her arms.

She yawned, her mouth opening wide and the air rushing into her lungs. She stretched again, her whole body tensing and flexing to send the blood coursing through veins and arteries.

The waking-up process took almost five minutes and by the time she clambered out of bed she was fully awake with her eyes wide open. She wondered where in hell Ralph might be.

It would have been nice to have him around, she decided. She loved sex in the morning, especially when you were still half awake and half asleep. Then you came together without preliminaries, almost like animals, two bodies reaching and straining for each other and possessing each other without the brains getting in the way.

It was good in the morning.

But Ralph wasn't around—and, unfortunately, neither was anyone else. She hurried into the bathroom for a shower and turned on the water. Then she kicked off her slippers and climbed into the small bathtub.

A shower, like everything else she enjoyed, was a sensual experience for Stella. She didn't just soap her body and rinse it. Instead she caressed herself with the soap, loving the smooth and slippery way it passed over her body.

She loved to soap her breasts. She kneaded the lather into the soft smooth skin in a manner that was almost physically arousing. She did the same for all the erogenous zones of her perfect body.

Then, when she was through, she turned on the cold shower full blast. Needles of icy liquid pain pelted her all over and hurt her in a deliciously invigorating way. The freezing water lashed at her breasts and belly and made her even more aware of herself.

When she had stepped out of the tub and toweled herself dry she stood for almost fifteen minutes before her mirror. She loved to spend time at her mirror; she had done so since she was a small child.

Stella had developed early. Her breasts began to grow when she was only eleven years old and reached their full size by the time she was fourteen. She was never physically awkward the way so many adolescent girls are. She grew from a pretty child to a beautiful woman with no unpleasant period of transition.

And since she was eleven she would spend time before the mirror, looking at her reflection and admiring it. She would cup her breasts and squeeze them gently, telling herself that they were beautiful. She would strike poses before the mirror and study the effect at great length.

Both her early development and her strong basic sex drives had a good deal to do with the course of her life. Stella's father had been a doctor in Bay Shore and he had made a good deal of money. Her mother, who was a few years older than her husband, died of throat cancer while Stella was still in grade school. Her parents had been very close to one another and the shock ruined her father. He tended to blame himself for it. Since he was a doctor himself, he argued that he should have made certain his wife had periodic physical examinations which might have caught the disease in time, before it was too late.

And so he began to drink. His practice went quietly to hell and he spent all his time by himself in the room where he and Stella's mother had lived, drinking bonded bourbon from an Old Fashioned glass and talking softly to himself. Stella was on her own by the time she was twelve—not on her own like a slum child, for she had plenty of money and a good home. On her own in that there was no one to take care of her, no one to talk to her, no one to love her.

And she needed love, needed it desperately. She sought love wherever it was available, but the empty, vacant atmosphere that was her home turned love to sex and emotion to passion. Love fell by the wayside; Stella never did find out what it really meant.

But she slept with a lot of people.

She approached sex the way that she approached life in general—bluntly, directly, and solely in her own self-interest. She took whatever she wanted and she wanted nearly everything.

Her father died shortly after she entered high school. Both high school and the three years she spent in college were a chore for her. She already knew precisely how she wanted to spend the rest of her life, and she didn't need a college diploma in order to carry through with her plans.

The income from her father's estate came to a little over twelve thousand dollars a year. While this didn't make her really wealthy, it meant that she could lead a life of complete and total leisure, never working and never doing anything other than what she wanted to do. And this was fine with Stella James.

She moved to the Village, the one place where she was sure she could live as she pleased with no outside interference. She took lovers when she wanted them. That was her life and she enjoyed it.

Sometimes—but not very often—a vague feeling would pass through her mind that she was missing something, that her life was a waste and that the world she lived in was an empty one. The thought was essentially disturbing, and she fought that thought as she fought anything which threatened to disturb the relative security of her existence.

She found a new person to make love to or a new way to make love.

The thought was passing through her mind then as she looked at her body in the mirror. She remembered the previous night and something about it bothered her. It seemed as though every sexual encounter of late was getting just so much more depraved and twisted. Ordinarily this didn't bother her; she looked upon perversion and depravity as the natural outgrowth of sex.

But something seemed wrong. She had to do something to make herself feel better.

She knew what to do.

Humming softly to herself she went to the bedroom and dressed quickly. Then she returned to the living room and picked up the receiver of the phone. She made herself comfortable on the couch and dialed a number.

After several rings a man's voice said, "Hello."

"Jimmy?"

"Speaking."

"This is Stella James, Jimmy."

"Hi, honey. What can I do for you?"

"I'm having a party," she said. "Tonight. I wondered if you'd like to come."

"Love to. I've never missed a party of yours yet, have I?"

"Swell. Drop up about nine."

"Will do."

"And Jimmy—"

"Yeah?"

"Bring some stuff," she said. "You know what I mean."

"Gotcha. How much?"

"Enough for about a dozen people," she said. "We'll have a real blast."

She hung up and relaxed on the couch, smiling happily to herself. Then she lifted the receiver again and dialed another number.

"I'd like to paint you some time," Ralph said.

"Maybe," she said. "Maybe sometime."

"I mean it, Susan. You're a very lovely girl." She looked away.

"This isn't a line," he went on. "And I enjoy being with you. Hell, you've broken down my painter's block. This is the first time I've felt like painting anything in a long while."

"I've never posed before, Ralph."

"That doesn't matter."

"I probably wouldn't be a very good model."

"You'll be all right."

She thought for a moment. "Where would you do it? Your apartment?"

"If there's no place better. The lighting's kind of weak. What floor are you on?"

"Fourth floor front. Why?"

"You get a good north light there," he explained. "I could paint there, if you'd let me. It would be a lot better than my place."

She nodded absently. Then she took a puff of her cigarette and studied the glowing tip of it for a moment before she spoke.

"Ralph," she said, "how would you paint me?"

"In oils."

"I know that. I mean . . . nude?"

"Not if you'd rather not, if you prefer I'll do a head and shoulders study of you. But I'd rather do you full figure, with or without clothes. Your head and your body go very well together."

"They've been together a long time."

He laughed. "That's not what I meant. An artist looks at everything a little bit differently, especially people. Sometimes the various parts of a person complement each other more than other times. Your particular head looks better attached to your particular body, and vice-versa."

"Naturally," she said. "Either of them would look kind of silly just rolling around by themselves."

"That's not what I—"

She laughed, delighted. "I know what you meant, silly. I was just teasing you. But I do think it might be nice to pose for you, if you really want me to."

"I do."

"I will, then—and we can use my apartment if you'd rather. I think I might be embarrassed posing at your place anyway."

"Whatever way you want it."

"And . . . Ralph?"

"What, Susan?"

She closed her eyes for a minute. Then she opened them and said, "I know you told me before that you weren't a guy on the make. But I have to make sure, Ralph. I . . . I'm not looking for anything remotely resembling a sexual relationship. Not for the time being and not for the foreseeable future."

"I understand."

"I don't want to keep harping away at this," she went on. "It's just that this is such a standard set-up in the Village. Village artist meets Village girl and asks her to pose for him and they go to an apartment and crawl into a bed. I don't think that's what you want but I want to get everything set straight at the beginning so that neither of us will be disappointed."

"I understand," he said again. "Besides, there's already a girl. I told you."

"I know. But down here it's not too uncommon for a person to be sleeping with more than one person at the same time."

Thanks for telling me, he thought, thinking of Stella.

"But I really would like to pose for you," she said. "I like you, Ralph. As a person, I mean. I like you very much and I think I'd enjoy getting to know you better. But only as a person."

"I like you, too, Susan. We hit it off pretty well together. I usually have trouble talking to people."

She smiled softly. "So do I. But I want to emphasize that no matter how well I get to know you or how much I get to like you, our relationship will have to stay on a purely platonic level. Just friends."

"Okay," he said. "And I'm just as glad that you put everything out in the open at the start. Down here if a guy doesn't make a pass at a girl the first day he meets her she feels insulted, or else thinks he's a fruit or something. If you hadn't said something I might have had to throw you a pass just to keep up appearances."

"Don't ever do that. Maybe we'll be very good friends, Ralph. That's a rare enough thing."

"Right," he said. "Hello, friend."

"Hi," she said. "Hi, friend."

She insisted on paying half the check. Then they left the restaurant and walked back to 69 Barrow Street, walking slowly with the sun beating down on them. Ralph glanced at his watch and noted that it was close to noon. Where had the time gone to? Evidently they had been talking for quite a while.

The traffic was getting heavier and he could hear trucks and buses rolling by on Seventh Avenue. Barrow Street was filled with neighborhood children playing the myriad games that children played in New York, where there was no place to play but the street. Stickball, stoop ball, Chinese handball—the kids never seemed to tire of the street games, never lacked a way to amuse themselves.

Just like Stella, he thought. *She can always find a way to amuse herself. And it's usually in a horizontal position.*

Not always horizontal, he realized. Stella had a marvelous imagination.

At 69 Barrow he opened the door for Susan and followed her inside. They said goodbye at the staircase and he returned to the door of his apartment, fitting the key in the lock.

He listened to Susan's footsteps on the staircase for several seconds before turning the key and entering his apartment.

CHAPTER 3

Stella was smiling when he walked into the apartment.

"Well," she said. "Two-timing me, huh?"

"What do you mean?"

"Just now. With the little brunette."

"Oh," he said. "The two of us had breakfast together. She just moved into the building."

"Sort of a long breakfast, wasn't it?"

"We were talking for a while," he said defensively. There was nothing for him to be defensive about, but Stella had the knack of making him feel guilty for no reason whatsoever.

"What's her name?"

"Susan Rivers."

"She's very pretty, Ralph."

"I know. I'm thinking of doing a painting of her. That's what we were talking about."

Stella pouted. "You don't want to paint me anymore?"

"I just wanted to try something different."

"That's all right," she said quickly. "I don't really mind. As a matter of fact, I intend to get to know the girl myself."

He looked at her, puzzled.

"You see," she went on, "we've met before. She's the one I was telling you about yesterday. The one I intend to take to bed sometime in the very near future. Susan Rivers, you said? I'll have to remember her name."

His mouth dropped open but no words came out. Stella looked at him for a moment and suddenly burst out in harsh, strident laughter.

"You mean you didn't know? You couldn't tell?"

"You're crazy!"

"You couldn't tell!" Her eyes were laughing at him. "My God, Ralph—why, it stands out all over her. She's so obviously gay I'm amazed you didn't spot her right away."

"Stella—"

"You're a real artist, aren't you? One look at a person and you can tell things other people wouldn't notice. But anything that's perfectly straightforward and obvious sails right past you."

"Stella," he said again. "Stella, I don't want you to bother that girl."

"*Bother* her?"

"You know what I mean."

"Why don't you say what you mean? There's a better word than bother for what I had in mind."

"I want you to leave her alone," he said. "She doesn't want you."

"You're wrong, Ralph."

"She doesn't. And I want you to leave her be. Do you understand me?"

"Of course I understand. That doesn't mean I'm going to listen to the nonsense you're spouting. What in the world's got into you, anyway? Have you fallen for our little Miss Rivers? That won't matter. You can have a crack at her when I'm done—"

"Shut up!"

She grinned. "You know, I think that's it. You're in love with her!"

"Don't be silly."

"You must be. You're a real nut, Ralph—falling in love with a dyke."

"You're being ridiculous," he said, frowning. "I like her, that's all. Even if she is a lesbian, she's one hell of a nice person—which is something you'd never understand. And I don't want you to get your hooks into her, Stella. You ruin people. You turn them all rotten inside."

She crossed her legs and reached for a cigarette. "Aren't you being a little too dramatic, dear? Whom did I ever ruin?"

He stared at her.

"Tell me. I'd like to know."

"Leave me alone, will you?"

She stood up and walked to him, pressing up against him and putting her arms around his neck. He tried to brush her away but she clung to him.

"Come on," she said. "Tell me who I've been ruining."

"Me," he said brokenly. "You've made a mess out of me. How's that for a starter?"

He expected her to laugh but this time she didn't. Instead she released him and took a step backwards. There was a new expression in her eyes, a mixture of pity and contempt.

"You really think I ruined you?"

He nodded, not looking at her.

"No," she said. "Not me, Ralph. You were a wreck before I ever laid eyes on you."

•   •   •

Susan Rivers read the same paragraph three times in succession.

The third time around she realized that the paragraph seemed familiar. She closed her eyes for a second and came to the realization that it had taken her twenty minutes to read five pages of the book she held in her hand. And on top of that she could no longer remember anything that had been on any of the five pages.

Disgusted, she closed the book and returned it to the bookshelf. She curled up in the mammoth armchair, the only really nice piece of furniture in the apartment, and tried to force herself to relax.

It didn't work. It never worked. There were some things you couldn't force on yourself, and relaxation happened to be one of them.

She closed her eyes once again and thought about Ralph Lambert. It was, all things considered, quite pleasant to think about Ralph Lambert. He was nice company. And she didn't seem to feel afraid of him.

With most men she was afraid, almost petrified. Not with gay men, of course, and she had been quite friendly with one or two of them from time to time. But a friendship with a male homosexual was never particularly satisfying. It seemed forced, as if the two of them were friends primarily because homosexuality served as a common bond.

Men who were straight generally frightened her. The thought of a man touching her with his coarse hands, forcing her and hurting her, bending her down onto a bed and kissing her, touching all the private parts of her body and then . . . then . . .

When she opened her eyes she realized that she had been shivering with fear and disgust.

But with Ralph she felt comfortable, and she hoped that he wouldn't try to change their friendship into anything sexual. Not only was he a man, but she was fairly certain that the woman he was living with was the woman she had passed the day before on the stoop, the woman she had found so damnably attractive.

Would anything come of her attraction for the woman? Half of her being hoped the two of them would have an affair, if only a brief one. The other half prayed that they would live their separate lives and that their paths would never cross in any manner more intense than an occasional meeting in the hallway. While she wanted the woman, sexual involvement of any sort was one thing she desired desperately to avoid for the time being.

Susan had been a lesbian for almost two years, a relatively short time. In the course of those two years she had made love with six women. The six affairs ranged in duration from five months with Gloria to one night with a girl named Alicia whom she had met in a Village bar. She remembered the first time—it seemed so long ago, and yet it all happened less than two years ago, just a month before her twenty-second birthday. Perhaps she had been a lesbian before that without knowing it; the fact that she had avoided any sexual relationship with men on a deep level suggested that to her. But the first real affair began in September, several months after her graduation from art school.

She had spent the summer as arts and crafts counselor at a summer camp in the Catskills, and when she hit the city she had nothing to do and no place to go. She wanted to get some sort of job that would let her continue with her work in ceramics, but jobs of that type didn't grow on trees. So she lived with her parents in the Flatbush section of Brooklyn, read the Help Wanted ads every morning in the *Times*, and spent her evenings strolling around Greenwich Village, drinking *cafe espresso* in the little coffee houses, listening to modern jazz in a dimly lit bar and watching people feeding pigeons in Washington Square.

It was on one of those evenings that she met Sharon. She and Sharon had been in art school together. Sharon was a year or so older and the two of them had never been very friendly, knowing each other well enough to exchange nods in the hallway but not much more than that. But when she met the older girl in the Village, Sharon gave her a heavy welcome and Susan was lonely enough to be grateful.

They went out drinking in a quiet bar; she couldn't remember anymore which bar it had been. It was a warm evening and they drank dry martinis on the rocks. The drinks were very refreshing and very cool and very effective, and Susan had never been much of a drinker to begin with.

She got quite high in a short amount of time.

Thinking back, she couldn't remember whether Sharon had told her she was a lesbian before or after they went to the older girl's apartment. Probably after, because she probably would have refused to go if she had known.

At Sharon's apartment, a little one-room-with-kitchenette place on Bank Street, everything happened with phenomenal speed. The first part was not fresh anymore in her mind, but she remembered that almost as soon as they were inside the door Sharon was kissing her, covering her mouth with lips that were soft and tender and sweet. And what followed, followed swiftly, with

Sharon pressing her down on the bed without even bothering to remove the spread, pressing her down and lying on top of her and grinding her body into hers. It had ended almost before it began.

Then they were lying together on the bed, with Sharon's long red hair hanging to her waist and contrasting beautifully with her pale, milky skin. Susan was in a state of shock at the time, numb with the liquor and even more numb with the realization of what she had done. And Sharon had explained to her exactly what she was and what they had done, and the sort of life she could expect to lead in the future.

And then the second time. "I want to make it good for you," Sharon said. "Lie down and be perfectly still and don't move at all. Don't even think about anything, darling. Or if you must, tell yourself that you love me."

She did as she was told. She lay down on her back with her head resting gently on a soft foam-rubber pillow. She closed her eyes and let her mind go completely blank, concentrating entirely on the physical sensations that came to her and letting her whole body respond to them.

Sharon began to kiss her. Her lips touched Susan's eyelids first, kissing them in turn. The mere touch of the other girl's lips on her eyelids seemed to relax Susan. She breathed deeply.

Then Sharon's mouth fastened on her mouth and Sharon's tongue darted out and slipped between her lips, licking and caressing the inside of her mouth. It was like no kiss she had ever experienced before. The whole inside of her mouth began to tingle and she could sense the blood coursing through her body. Sharon kissed her again. Then her lips darted to Susan's throat and she kissed her all over her neck, little fast kisses that gave her a warm heady feeling.

Sharon's fingertips toyed with the younger girl's breasts. Susan's first impulse was to shrink away, but the touch was so pleasant, so gentle and delightful, that instead she found herself responding. Then Sharon's lips moved to the cleft between her breasts while her hands continued their gentle caressing.

Then Sharon put her mouth to each of Susan's breasts in turn. She covered every square inch of the smooth, lightly tanned flesh with kisses and Susan hadn't believed that such extraordinarily marvelous sensations existed. Sharon bathed each of her breasts completely with her hot, insistent tongue and Susan began to breathe very quickly. She couldn't keep her feet still as the passion flooded her brain and her body began to writhe sensuously on the bed.

Sharon continued to kiss her. Her hungry mouth moved lower.

Lower . . .

It was perfect.

That whole night had been perfect. After they had made love that second time she drifted off to a deep sleep with her head pressed tightly to Sharon's breast. Then, hours later, she woke up and Sharon cooked breakfast for the two of them.

Then they went back to bed.

The next day she explained to her parents that she had found an apartment in the Village that she was going to share with a girl from school. She moved in with Sharon.

They made love almost constantly for the first few weeks. Sharon had been involved in lesbianism for years, ever since her French teacher had managed to seduce her during her second year in high school. She knew just about everything there was to know about the technical side of lesbianism and the mechanics of it. She told Susan a great deal and showed her even more.

They remained together for three and a half months. Then they drifted apart. They had nothing in common, really, except for their attraction to one another. When the freshness of their love wore off, they separated and Susan found a room of her own on West Tenth Street. About the same time she managed to get work in the ceramics shop where she was still employed. At the beginning she worked behind the counter, but when the man who ran the shop saw the work she was capable of doing he put her in the workroom. At first he designed the objects she was to make; then he began to let her work out some designs on her own.

She was a happy person, all things considered. She enjoyed her work tremendously and enjoyed living in the Village. It was sort of a small town within the larger city, and the free and easy air about it appealed to her.

At times her lesbianism bothered her. She had always been fond of children, for example, and the knowledge that she would never have children of her own was disturbing. While she herself felt that "normal" sex was simply the name given to the sexual practice which happened to be followed by the majority of the world, and that there was no such thing as a perversion, her abnormality periodically annoyed her.

And there were times when she wondered what would have

become of her if she hadn't met Sharon that night. Would she have drifted to lesbianism regardless? Perhaps, but there was also the possibility that it would never have occurred to her. Then what would have happened?

She guessed that she would have lived alone by herself for a long time—several years at least. Then she would have met a man and married him in time. She could picture herself living a normal life without ever suspecting she was abnormal.

But how unhappy she would have been!

She never would have been able to enjoy sex with her husband. That was certain. Even if she could have managed to let him make love to her—a thought which in itself was so terrifying and so repugnant to her that it made her shake—she could never have derived any pleasure from the act. She would have completely missed the pleasure she received from Sharon, and that pleasure alone more than compensated for the occasional feelings of distress over her abnormality.

Her thoughts returned to Ralph Lambert. Except for sex, he was the type of man she might have been able to stand being married to. She certainly didn't *dislike* men, the way so many lesbians did. In fact she had always preferred the companionship of men to that of women, except that men frightened her so much.

But she wasn't afraid of Ralph. It had been a good idea to put it to him right from the beginning—no sex, now or later. And he didn't seem to take offense, either. He evidently liked her for herself, as a person.

But he appreciated her as a woman, too. She could tell that readily enough. While he never stared at her with naked hunger in his eyes, the admiration of her face and body was easy to recognize. And it was a good deal stronger than the admiration of an artist for a beautiful object. Ralph hadn't looked at her with the eyes of a lecher, but he hadn't gazed at her as he might have gazed at a beautiful landscape either.

She hoped they would continue to get along. What would it be like posing for him? She could hardly imagine it. It would certainly be strange, holding a pose while a man tried to reproduce her on a canvas. And even if the man was a man she knew, even if he was Ralph, she wasn't sure whether she would be able to pose nude for him.

She thought back to their conversation and giggled. At any rate, it was nice to know that her head and body went well together!

Ralph hauled one of the colonial chairs over to the front window and sat down in it. His eyes stared out the window toward Barrow Street but he wasn't conscious of anything that he saw there.

His mind was elsewhere.

He wondered how much truth was contained in Stella's last statement. *You were a wreck before I ever laid eyes on you*, she had said. At first it had sounded to him like a typical statement of hers, defending by attacking. She said things of that nature frequently, as if she could make herself less vile by dragging everybody down to her own level.

But perhaps there was more than a grain of truth in what she had said. Maybe he was no good from the start. Maybe he had made a mess out of his own life, and had only himself to blame for his current state of affairs. Stella was obviously a corrupting influence—hell, a woman like her would exert a corrupting influence on Satan himself. But maybe he was already pretty corrupt when she came into his life.

What had he been like before Stella James?

It was hard to remember. It was hard to visualize any life for himself other than the one he lived now, hard to picture himself in any surroundings other than those of the Village, hard to imagine him living anyplace beside 69 Barrow Street or with anybody but Stella James.

But there had been times before that. What sort of life had he led then?

He forced himself to go over his life briefly. Childhood in Xenia, Ohio—that had been uneventful enough, with nothing and nobody in that little hickish town to excite or stimulate him. The local college where he majored in art. Then two years in the army, and all he could remember about those days was that he hated them—the monotony, the drabness, the regimented life where he had to bow and scrape before authority and do the same boring tasks day after day after day. If he had been a cartoonist or an illustrator it wouldn't have been so bad; he could have done something fairly interesting during his hitch in the service. As it was he sweated out the time as a clerk in Fort Polk, Louisiana, typing report after report and spending his nights drinking or playing cards or sacked out with one of the local prostitutes.

And then what? Then New York—with no job and nothing to his credit but ambitions. He thought he was a painter, but maybe he was wrong. Maybe he was just a bum who was throwing paint at canvas while he ran his way through his mustering-out pay and the few bucks his folks sent from home.

Maybe Stella had hit the nail on the head. Maybe he was a bum from the word go and living with Stella was just another step down the primrose path to hell, just another step closer to the ultimate in depravity and total and complete degradation.

No, by God, he had been a painter! He had never sold a painting, but his work was good, damned good! For confirmation he stood up and walked to the closet. On the top shelf was the nude he had done of Stella, the only painting he had in New York. The rest he had shipped home to Xenia or destroyed.

He took down the painting and set it up on the couch, stepping back a few paces to look at it. It was done in a mockery of the classic style much as was Manet's *Olympia,* a burlesque of the standard picture of Venus. Stella was posed on the couch, the same couch that the painting was propped up on now. She was completely nude. Like Venus, one hand supported her head while the other covered her groin from sight.

At that point the similarity between the two paintings ended. The one of Venus was seductive but pure at the same time; Ralph's painting attempted to capture the full character of Stella on canvas and succeeded admirably. Evil oozed forth unmistakably from every dab of paint on the canvas.

The smile on Stella's face was Satanic. There was cruelty shining forth from her eyes, cruelty in the lines at the corners of her mouth. The way she covered herself with her hand served not to conceal the area, as it did in the original painting, but to draw attention to it. Ralph had been very careful to make the area covered by the hand the dominant spot in the picture and he had managed to highlight it perfectly. Stella seemed to be offering herself in the very act of concealment.

Even the pose of her body was obscene. The soft flesh tones he had used to paint her were not only beautiful but tremendously sensual. By a clever use of long brushstrokes on her thighs and calves he had given the illusion of an immense amount of power, evil power, lustful power. Similarly, short and strong brushstrokes around her breasts made the breasts even more prominent than they deserved to be and accentuated the feeling of corruption and dissipation that emanated from the canvas.

He could not look at it without having to catch his breath. It was Stella, to be sure. More than that, it was one hell of a good picture. He had no doubt that he could sell it, but it was the one picture he had ever painted that he wanted to keep for himself. He wouldn't even hang it on the wall; he wanted to keep it hidden in the closet and take it out from time to time to look at by himself.

No, he hadn't been a wreck when she met him. He certainly hadn't arrived at the top or anywhere near the top, but he had the talent to make the grade.

Maybe he could still make it.

He thought about the painting he was going to do of Susan Rivers. She would make a fine model. She was certainly a lovely thing, but beauty itself had little to do with a subject's suitability. There had to be something else. The features of the model had to reflect something inside, some inner quality which the artist could transpose into color and shadow and line. Otherwise he might just as well take her picture with a camera—a camera certainly did a better job of getting a likeness. A picture had to do more. It had to say something.

Susan Rivers. He wondered if Stella was right and the girl was a lesbian. It was a strong possibility. Stella seldom made mistakes, and if it was true, it would explain the way she emphasized keeping things on a platonic basis. Well, that was all right with him. The girl had a right to live her own life and it was none of his business if she preferred to go to bed with girls.

Still, he hoped to god Stella stayed away from her. Stella was poison to anybody, man or woman. And Susan was such a sweet girl, such a remarkably nice person.

Stella would be bad for her.

When he heard Stella coming toward the room he hastily replaced the painting on the shelf and closed the closet door. She had seen the painting before, of course, but he didn't want her to see him looking at it. She would just make some wisecrack and they'd be arguing again.

She came into the room and flashed him a smile.

"I'm having a party tonight," she said.

"What kind of a party?"

"Don't you know?"

He knew, of course. It would be the kind of party she always had, the kind of party that made a Roman orgy look like a garden party on Long Island by comparison. His stomach turned over at the thought of it.

"Just a small get-together," she continued. "I'm having an even dozen people. Jimmy is bringing the stuff."

"Jimmy who and what stuff?"

"Jimmy is Jimmy Henderson. The stuff is marijuana."

He closed his eyes. "Count me out."

"Don't be ridiculous."

"I said count me out. If you think I'm coming to one more of those pot-smoking scenes of yours, you're out of your head."

"You've enjoyed them before."

"Only when I've been high. When it wore off I realized how sick the whole thing was. I'm not coming."

"You're certain?"

"Positive. I'll go out and find a bar to get quietly drunk in."

"All right, if that's the way you want it."

"That's precisely the way I want it."

"Fine," she said. "But that'll leave us one short. I'll have to ask your little girlfriend."

"Who?"

"Your girlfriend—the one you ate breakfast with. Susan Rivers, I think you said her name was."

"Don't ask her, Stella." His voice was flat and devoid of emotion.

"But I'll *have* to, darling. Otherwise we'll be one person short. And I'm sure she'll be delighted to come. She'll probably have a marvelous time."

"I don't want you to ask her, Stella."

She looked across the room at him, a smile on her face. "You mean you'll be coming to the party?"

He shut his eyes. Then he opened them again, defeated. "All right," he said. "I'll be coming to the party."

Chapter 4

Between 9 and 9:30 that evening five men and five women opened the outer door at 69 Barrow Street. In turn they pushed the buzzer in the vestibule marked *James Lambert,* walked through into the hallway and waited for Stella to let them into the first-floor apartment.

At first glance they appeared to be just a normal crowd of people between the ages of twenty and thirty. They were dressed informally, but there was nothing striking about their appearances, nothing that would indicate Bohemianism or non-conformity of any sort. They looked extremely average—a nice, quiet crowd of young people getting together for a few drinks and a good time.

But Ralph knew better.

He had met them all before. All of them had been to previous parties of Stella's. In addition, more than a few had been Stella's sexual partners.

Ralph knew them all quite well.

Jimmy and Rhonda Henderson sat together on the couch sipping drinks from water tumblers. Jimmy's black hair was clipped close to a large skull that teetered precariously on his small, thin frame. Small, piggish eyes stared out from his head and surveyed the room. Rhonda, who had married him when she woke up one morning and found herself pregnant, was a soft honey blonde with huge eyes and creamy skin. She stood several inches taller than Jimmy. It wasn't hard to tell by a glance at Rhonda that she was an extremely stupid girl. Her eyes had a perpetually vacant stare and her conversation was, to say the least, uninspired. There was, in fact, only one thing Rhonda could do at all well. But she was an expert at it.

Jimmy made his living—a rather good living—peddling marijuana. A good list of steady customers left him with around $300 a week after he paid off the local patrolman. While Stella bought too little marijuana to rank as a good customer, a sale to her meant an invitation to one of her parties. And he liked Stella's parties.

Near the window a very tall and very thin young man stood with his arm around a short, plump girl. The thin young man's name was Roger Brann. The plump girl was Sally; nobody knew her last name. Neither of them had jobs.

They had been living together for several months on their unemployment checks.

Roger Brann was 22 years old.

Sally was almost 16.

Ralph sat alone by himself, avoiding the others. In the background weird modern jazz played on Stella's hi-fi, filling the room with strangely erotic rhythms and harmonies.

Stella was talking earnestly with two other couples—David and Elaine Jordan and Luke and Betty Swinnerton. The Jordans started out as just an ordinary married couple, until they both decided that there was something lacking in ordinary married life. They got involved in a few minor wife-swapping deals with men who worked in the same advertising agency as David. Then they discovered the Village and Stella's crowd and their problems were solved. They were still very happily married, very much in love with each other. They looked upon the sexual experimentation of the Village as a release, a way to let off steam and to keep their own marriage fresh and exciting.

The Swinnertons, although both under thirty, had always seemed a little older than the other people in the room. It was hard for Ralph to determine just why this was true. He decided that it was in the way they pursued their "kicks." The others in the room approached depravity and dissipation in a madcap search for pleasure, hungrily chasing down every possible escape they could find. Luke and Betty were different. Like the Hendersons, they had married when Betty thought she was pregnant. In their case it turned out to be a fake pregnancy but they remained married when they found out it was more or less the same as living together. And when Luke and Betty looked for kicks they did it in a totally dispassionate way, as though they had already given up all hope of achieving any genuine happiness. They continued to dissipate because it was their life, the only life they had known for years. But nothing touched them and nothing moved them.

They stood talking to Stella and the Jordans, but they seemed a million miles removed from the conversation. There was a hollow stare in Luke's eyes. Betty kept her eyes closed and shifted her weight from one foot to the other, snapping her fingers absently in time to the music, humming softly to herself.

One other couple remained—Larry Colestock and Maria Raines. The two of them shared a cold-water flat on the East Side off Third Avenue. Ralph didn't know Larry well at all, but he would never forget Maria, with her large, brown eyes and jet-black, shoulder length hair.

He had met her at another party of Stella's, two or three months ago. Stella had met her and invited her to the party, and when she came Stella slipped a powder into the girl's drink.

The powder was called Spanish Fly.

Maria had been a virgin. That night Stella led the little girl to the bedroom in back and ten men, one after the other, put an end to Maria's virginity and ripped away her self-respect as they tore her inside. Then, when the men had finished with the girl, Stella took her in her strong arms and held her close for the remainder of the night.

That had been either the beginning or the end of Maria, depending on how you looked at it. She left her family and moved permanently to the Village. Looking vaguely for love, she took whatever happened to come her way. Nothing mattered to her any more.

A wave of shame washed over Ralph.

He had been one of the ten men that night.

Stella walked to the window and pulled the shade all the way down. While she didn't mind at all if passers-by watched Ralph make love to her, there were certain things that she didn't want anybody to see. Then she walked to the middle of the room and held up a hand for silence.

"All right," she said. "Okay, everybody. It's time for us to get started. You got everything, Jimmy?"

Henderson nodded. He took a small, bulging envelope from his pocket and handed it to her. Stella ripped open the envelope and dumped the contents into the palm of her right hand.

The joints were about one-third the thickness of a regular cigarette. The ends were twisted to keep the weed from spilling out. Stella counted the joints, unable to keep the anticipation from showing on her face as she did so. Then she picked one up between the thumb and forefinger of her left hand and examined it carefully.

"Twelve of them," she announced. "Twelve bombers. Enough to knock us out of our heads."

There was a low murmur of approval from the others.

"C'mon," she said. "Everybody get seated in a circle on the floor and we'll get the ball rolling."

The group formed a circle on the large oriental rug. Ralph found himself seated between Maria Raines and Elaine Jordan. He wished fleetingly that he was somewhere else, anywhere but here. He liked marijuana, enjoyed the effect it had on him, but he knew what it would do to the party.

Stella put the first of the cigarettes between her lips and accepted a light from Henderson. She dragged deeply on the joint with her lips slightly parted so that she would smoke it properly, taking in a mixture of air and smoke. She drew the mixture directly into her lungs in order to get the maximum effect, rather than puffing on it and then inhaling as with a regular cigarette. In this way the maximum amount of smoke was absorbed into the bloodstream and the greatest possible effect achieved.

As soon as she had finished dragging on the joint she passed it to Henderson. By keeping the cigarette moving around the circle less of the smoke was lost than if each person smoked a joint by himself. She held the smoke in her lungs as long as possible.

When she let out her breath she was smiling.

"Cool," she murmured. "Deep."

Stella was getting the second joint going by the time the first one reached Ralph. He took it between the thumb and forefinger of his right hand and brought it to his lips. Despite his misgivings, the sharp odor of marijuana present in the room had made him anxious to turn on, to smoke some of the pot and get high.

He sucked greedily on the joint and tasted the familiar taste of the marijuana, felt the familiar sting as the hot smoke scorched his throat and lungs. He took in as much smoke as he could hold and passed the joint to Elaine. Then he let his eyelids drop shut as he felt the marijuana hit home.

By the time he breathed out Maria was handing him the second joint. He repeated the process. This time the smoke caused less pain to his throat and lungs and he could feel the drug beginning to work, loosening him up and increasing his sensory perceptions. His mind felt much clearer and he could close his eyes and become very conscious of all the organs in his body. He heard his heart pounding out a firm, steady rhythm, felt the blood coursing through veins and arteries, listened to the contraction and relaxation of muscles when he moved his fingers.

One by one they smoked the twelve joints. When the cigarettes had burned down so far that they couldn't be smoked any longer they were extinguished, and what remained was known as the roach. Henderson walked around the circle, his beady eyes gleaming unnaturally, and passed out a roach to each of the smokers. They each removed some of the tobacco from the end of a regular cigarette and stuffed in the roach, twisting the end of the cigarette to keep it in place.

Then the roaches were smoked. It was like the slaughterhouses in Chicago, where they boast of using "all of the pig but the squeal." Not a grain of the precious marijuana was wasted.

Ralph was very high, higher than he had been in months. He remained on the floor with his legs out in front of him and his eyes closed. Everything felt so good, so perfectly peaceful. Nothing mattered anymore. To hell with Stella, to hell with Susan, to hell with everybody. He just didn't care about a thing, not a single thing.

He stood up precariously and surveyed the room. He felt completely at ease now. A voice—Stella's—suggested that all the girls strip to the waist, and he leaned up against the wall and watched as each of the women removed her blouse and bra, tossing the clothes to the floor.

He walked over to Elaine Jordan. She was talking to her husband and her back was turned to Ralph. He reached around her from the back and his hands closed over her huge breasts. Her breasts were very firm and the nipples were hard and warm. He moved closer to her and the perfume wafted from her soft brown hair to his nostrils. The marijuana, which made every sense stronger and more acute, made his sense of smell so sharp that her perfume tickled his nose.

Calmly, almost absently; he began to manipulate her breasts with his hands. She went on talking very intently to David, her husband, hardly even noticing what Ralph was doing, and he buried his face in her soft hair and went on caressing her breasts.

•　　　•　　　•

Stella slipped her arm around Luke Swinnerton's waist and let her breasts push against his chest. "What's the matter?" she asked. "You didn't seem to be getting any charge from the pot?"

"It's no kick for me anymore."

"How come?"

He shrugged.

"Tell me."

Silently he rolled up the sleeve of his left arm and showed her the arm. It was dotted with needle marks all the way up and down the main vein. Her eyes widened.

"Horse," he explained. "Heroin."

"How long?"

"A month, maybe two."

"Are you hooked?"

"Through the bag and back again."

"That's too bad. What does Betty think?"

Luke shrugged again. "She's hooked, too."

"You mean you got her started?"

Luke smiled sadly. "Betty's a good little chick. She figured if I was going to have a habit she wanted to keep me company. She's a good chick, you know?"

Maria took David Jordan by the hand and led him away from his wife. Elaine was still standing in the same position but now her eyes were closed. Ralph continued to stroke her breasts.

Maria said, "You want to make it with me?"

David's eyes travelled the length of her body. They took in the long black hair, the big brown eyes, the soft little breasts and the strong, golden thighs.

"Yeah," he said. "Yeah, that's a scene."

"Greek?"

"What do you mean?"

"Greek style," she explained. "That's how I feel like making it."

He shook his head.

"Aw, why not?"

"I don't like it."

"Come on." She took him by the hand again and tried to pull him toward the bedroom in the back. He resisted her.

"Why not?" she demanded.

"It's just not my scene. I'll make it French, if you want. I dig it that way."

"Larry and I did it like that this afternoon. I want to do it Greek style."

"Later," he said, freeing himself and dismissing her. "It's just not my scene."

Roger Brann caught Jimmy Henderson by the arm. Roger's hair had fallen over into his eyes and his lips were very pale.

"You seen Sally?" he demanded.

"She disappeared into the bedroom with Larry Colestock a minute or two ago."

"Little bitch."

"Hell, you don't expect her to stick with you all the time, do you?"

"Of course not."

"Then what's bugging you?"

"I don't know. She coulda told me." Jimmy laughed.

"Say," Roger said. "You know, sometimes I get pretty fed up with women."

Jimmy looked at him.

"You know what I mean?"

"I think so."

"Well? Are you interested?"

Jimmy thought for a moment. "What the hell," he said finally. "It'll be something new."

"You never done it before?"

Jimmy shook his head.

"Then c'mon. Maybe you'll dig it."

"Where'll we go?"

"Bedroom."

"Can't," Jimmy said. "Larry and Sally are in there. I just told you."

"Where, then?"

"I think the bathroom's empty."

Roger smiled. "So what are we waiting for?"

Sally took off her dress. She dropped it on the floor. She wasn't wearing anything underneath it.

"Hurry up," Larry said. "I can't wait much longer." She joined him on the bed. He pulled her to him and kissed her, his tongue slipping between her lips. She let out a little moan and put her arms around his neck.

"God," she said. She buried her face in his neck. "Oh Jesus God."

"What's the matter?"

"I just wish I could make it," she said. "That's all. That's all I want."

"What are you talking about?"

"I just wish I could make it. I like it but it never happens for me."

"Never?"

"Never."

"That's a bitch," he said. "Hell, you still got time though. How old are you, anyway?"

"Almost sixteen."

"That all?"

"Yeah."

"Then you got plenty of time. Lots of chicks, they're twenty-five before they get banged for the first time. You got no worries."

"I hope you're right."

He ran his hand down her back. She was plump, and he liked the feeling of plenty of soft feminine flesh under his hand.

"Hey," he said. "I got an idea."

"What?"

"You ever try it with you on top?"

"No. Why?"

"You might have a better chance of making it."

"Honest?"

"There's a chance."

"What the hell," she said. "A chance is a chance."

• • •

Ralph was still handling Elaine's breasts. She seemed totally removed to a dream world of her own and totally oblivious to his hands on her. He didn't care. He just wanted to stand there forever with his hands cooled by her soft flesh.

Maria tugged at his arm.

"What do you want?"

"You want to make it with me?"

He flushed, remembering the last time. That time she hadn't had to ask. She didn't have a chance to ask, for that matter.

He shrugged.

"Please, Ralph. I'm trying to find someone who'll make it Greek fashion."

"I don't want to."

"Why the hell not?"

"I'm busy."

"Busy? All you're doing is giving her a feel."

Ralph smiled. "Yeah, but it's one hell of a feel."

"Do it Greek with me and you can feel me at the same time."

"Go away, will you."

"You go to hell," she said, leaving him. "You go straight to hell."

Rhonda said, "If you're on junk, do you and Luke do anything anymore?"

"No," Betty said.

"That must be rough to take."

"It's not that bad."

"No kidding?"

"Well," she said, "he can't do it any more, what with the junk and all. Sometimes I want to, but it doesn't matter too much to me. Just being with him is enough."

"I guess so."

"It's a shame," Betty said. "Luke and I were good together, you know. Luke used to be wonderful in bed."

"I know."

"Huh?"

"It was a long time ago," Rhonda said. "Before the two of you even knew each other."

Betty relaxed.

"I wouldn't horn in on you now," Rhonda went on. "Even if I could. I know how you two feel about each other."

Betty got a dreamy smile on her face. "We've very much in love," she said.

"I know it."

"Very much in love. It's so good this way. He loves me and I love him and it's wonderful. We're both pretty lucky, when you stop to think."

Stella and David Jordan were on the couch. Her arms were around his neck and their mouths were glued together. He had one hand under her skirt.

"I want you," she said. "I want you bad."

He lowered his head and began kissing her on the breasts.

"Oh, God," she said. "I can't wait, David."

"Neither can I."

"Then come on."

"Where? There's somebody in the bedroom and the bathroom door's locked."

"What's the matter with right here?"

"Here?"

"Sure."

"Here? On the couch?"

"Why not?"

"People'll be watching."

"I don't care."

"You sure?"

"Of course I'm sure," she said. "I don't give a damn if the whole world is watching."

"What the hell," he said. "Let 'em watch."

Maria stood in the middle of the living room. She took off all her clothes and stood completely naked.

Nobody seemed to notice her.

"God damn it," she shouted. "Doesn't anybody want to make it Greek style?"

Nobody said anything.

"God damn it!"

Everybody ignored her.

"What a dull party," she said. "What a stinking dull party!"

She sat down on the floor and rested her head on her knees and started to cry.

•   •   •

Jimmy and Roger walked out of the bathroom. "Well? Did you like it?"

"It was a scene," Jimmy admitted.

"Yeah."

"I like it better with women, of course."

"Naturally. So do I."

"But it's another way to make it."

"That's how I look at it."

"And everything's worth a go at some time or other."

"That's the way I feel."

"Yeah," Jimmy said. "Well."

Sally was breathing deeply. She snuggled her head against Larry's chest and kissed him.

"Well, I'll be damned," she said. "I'll be double-damned."

"I told you it would happen. All you had to do was give it a chance."

"You were right."

"See? There's nothing wrong with you. You're as normal as anybody else. It was just a question of giving yourself enough time."

She fell silent.

Then she said, "Could I come and live with you?"

"Why?"

"I like it with you."

"How about Roger?"

"To hell with Roger."

He thought for a minute. "Okay. I'll tell Maria to move out. I was getting tired of her anyway."

"Good," she said.

"We're pretty good together," he said. "Maybe it'll work out okay."

Elaine Jordan seemed to be in a trance. Ralph held her still, his mind wandering into another world. The pot had hit him harder than he had expected and he wanted nothing more than what he had—his hands on Elaine's lovely breasts and his mind floating through space and time.

Slowly he began to come back to reality. His hands continued their play with her breasts but now the process was beginning to excite him.

He wanted her.

Gently he slipped his hands around her waist and unbuckled her skirt. It dropped to the floor. Then he hooked his fingers under the elastic band of her pink silk panties and pushed them down over her hips and thighs. They dropped to the floor also.

He ran his hands the full length of her body, realizing for the first time what a truly beautiful woman she was. His fingers explored every area of her.

He wanted her. He couldn't wait.

"Elaine," he said. "Elaine."

She was still in a trance.

"Elaine."

She mumbled something unintelligible.

"Elaine," he said. "Bend over, Elaine."

Maria was crying.

Jimmy sat down beside her, slipped an arm over her shoulder. "Hey," he said. "Why the waterworks?"

She looked up. "I want to make it and nobody wants to make it with me."

"You shoulda asked me."

Her eyes brightened. "You wanta make it?"

"Why not?"

"Greek style?"

"Sure," he said. "Why not?"

They walked toward the bedroom.

"Only one thing," he said. "Why Greek style? Isn't that pretty painful for a woman?"

"Of course," she said, puzzled. "Why else do you think I want to do it that way?"

The party didn't break up until 5:30 in the morning.

Chapter 5

It was well past noon when Ralph awoke and climbed out of bed over the still-asleep form of Stella. He yawned and stretched and reached for a cigarette. After the cigarette was lit and the first puff of smoke taken deep into his lungs he was able to think clearly.

But he didn't want to think clearly. He didn't want to think at all. He wanted to crawl back into the bed and pull the covers over his head and never come out. He didn't want to see anybody or do anything.

He felt sick inside, sick and weak and tormented. He closed his eyes so that he wouldn't have to look at Stella, but with his eyes closed other images, worse pictures, flooded his mind.

He opened his eyes again.

There are no physical after-effects from smoking marijuana. There is no hangover, no physical craving for the drug, no boggy feeling in the limbs or fuzziness in the brain such as frequently follows a good drinking bout. When the drug wears off, the user is right where he was when he started, right where he would have been if he had never smoked the stuff in the first place.

So he couldn't blame the way he felt on the marijuana. Ralph felt sick, physically sick, but not due to any physical causes. The memories of the party churned in his stomach and rose up in his throat and for a moment he thought he was going to be sick.

The moment passed.

Calmly he gazed around the small bedroom. Everything was in a frightening state of disarray. Feminine undergarments, some forgotten in the excitement of the evening and others torn to ribbons by the haste of the participants, covered the floor.

Ralph stooped over and picked up a tattered pair of lacy black panties. He stood up and held them in his hand, studying them. Vaguely he wondered whose they might have been and how they might have been reduced to their present torn state.

Well, it hardly mattered. Nothing mattered. Nothing could possibly matter, not when everything was so horribly sick and rotten inside.

Again his eyes scanned the room. Used contraceptives littered the floor, the castaways of those few couples who had cared enough to take precautions. Feeling his stomach beginning to turn over again, Ralph dressed in a hurry and left the room.

The front room was even worse. He sat down weakly on the couch and surveyed the damage. Most of the furniture was scarred with cigarettes that had been forgotten to burn themselves out on table tops. There was a large burn in the center of the oriental rug.

But worst of all was the memories that the room held.

How could he banish those memories from his mind? It would be hard enough to attempt to forget what he had seen, the dissipation and perversion and decadence, the switching of partners back and forth, over and over until at last the sun streamed through the window and the party came to a grinding halt.

But how could he forget what he had done?

How?

He made room for himself on the couch by pushing aside

some of the debris of the party and sat down heavily. His mind refused to focus properly and he lit a second cigarette from the butt of the first, chain-smoking in an effort to bring himself back to something with a vague resemblance to life.

To hell with it, he thought. To hell with trying anymore and to hell with pretending. He was no better than the rest of them, no better than Stella even. He was a sick, twisted little man and there was no point in pretending to be anything else. An artist? Sure, sure he was an artist. A pervert was more like it.

Now it would be very simple. He would stick to his life with Stella and he wouldn't complain anymore. He would let himself enjoy it. It could be an enjoyable life—if you threw morality and human decency to the winds and let yourself be led around by the sheer pursuit of pure physical pleasure and gratification.

And he could probably learn to appreciate a life like that. He was sick and perverted and twisted enough to begin with . . .

Anything would be better than what he had now. And once he relaxed and accepted himself for what he was things would be one hell of a lot easier. Life would be a constant ball with lots of things happening, and so what if he couldn't look at himself in the mirror without getting sick to his stomach? There were still a hell of a lot of kicks to try, still a countless number of women to make it with and a countless number of ways to make it.

Marijuana—as much as he wanted as often as he wanted it with no guilt feelings attached. Bennies and Dexies and goof-balls. Cough syrup with a high codeine content. Cocaine to sniff, heroin to sniff and to joy-pop.

So many ways.

Coke and snuff and aspirin. You mixed the three ingredients in a bowl and drank what you wound up with and got high on it.

Nutmeg. You took a spoonful of it and chewed it up and swallowed it and got high.

Mescaline. You took the peyote buds and cored them and chewed them up and swallowed them. They tasted terrible but after a while you managed to get them down and keep them down. And then for the next twelve hours you were in dreamland, entranced by the beauty in the folds of a piece of cloth, hearing colors and smelling music and seeing perfume, with all your senses joyfully confused and your appreciation of everything intensified beyond description.

So many kicks.

Too many kicks.

Too many kicks spoil the broth, he thought insanely. Too many kicks in the head break a man's spirit. Too many kicks in the . . .

He had to relax. He pitched his cigarette into the fake fireplace and stared at it.

Too many kicks.

He stood up. It was tempting, the notion of not pretending anymore, of letting himself go to hell completely. And perhaps it was the right thing to do, the course that was morally right as well as attractive. What did the word *perversion* mean, anyway? He knew that a good ninety percent of the sexual customs of the average human being were technically abnormal and quite often illegal. In his own home state, for example, almost anything the least bit different was against the law, although the laws were in fact never enforced. Ohio actually made any sort of intercourse virtually impossible due to a strange law prohibiting any person from touching the genitals of any other person—this law applied to married persons as well, and anybody who observed it would have one hell of a tough time doing much of anything.

A perversion, he decided, was only something that everybody wanted to do in secret but that very few people ever got around to doing. Almost any individual you could select had within him the basic desire to commit almost any act you could conceive of. If the average spinster schoolteacher got rid of her inhibitions for an hour or two she would be no better and no worse than a twisted, vicious woman like Stella.

But there had to be a difference. He thought suddenly of Susan Rivers, the girl he had met just yesterday. Was it only a day ago that he and Susan had met for breakfast? It seemed impossible. So much had happened since then, so much . . .

Stella had told him that the girl was a lesbian, and it was probably the truth. Stella had a second sense about things like that; she seldom made a mistake.

So Susan was probably a lesbian.

And that, of course, was a perversion.

But there was a difference between Susan and Stella. Christ, there had to be. There had to be some way of distinguishing between a deviation from the sexual norm and cruel, vicious decadence. Common human decency and kindness had to count for something. Anything a person did was all right, but when a person did things that hurt other people it stopped being permissible.

That had to be it.

He stood very still, his hands at his side and his mind working double-time. In the bedroom Stella was still asleep; he could hear her slow, rhythmic breathing. Outside on Barrow Street there were more people walking around than usual, but the street was still very quiet.

Ralph was thinking.

He couldn't let himself go to seed, not completely, not yet. There was still a chance that he could find a normal life for himself and he had to follow that chance up. He had to go to Susan, to paint her picture, to use his paints and brushes as the tools to dig his way back to a decent sort of an existence.

He still had a chance.

Hell, it wasn't much of a chance. Maybe he wouldn't be able to paint worth a damn any more. Maybe whatever talent he once possessed was gone now and he wouldn't be able to draw a straight line with a ruler. But as long as there was a chance he had to take it. As long as there was a single course open that might lead him out of the pitfall of perversion, that was the course he had to follow.

He walked to the closet and opened the door. On the top shelf with the painting of Stella was a small flat wooden box that contained his brushes and his tubes of paint. Next to the box was his palette, and beside it was a fresh canvas. He took them all down and laid them out on the couch.

His easel was standing on the floor of the closet behind several of Stella's coats. He took it out and shut the closet door again.

It was hard to carry all his paraphernalia at once but he managed. He loaded himself up and opened the apartment door. Then, not bothering to close the door, he walked to the staircase and began to mount the steps to the fourth floor.

Ralph didn't shut the door to his apartment.

Now normally he did shut the door. On this occasion, however, he was too encumbered with painting equipment to do so without putting all his things down and then picking them up again. This seemed a lot of trouble to go through just to shut a door, especially since Stella was home and since there was nothing much worth stealing in the apartment anyway and since it was mid-afternoon and a rather ridiculous time for a burglary. Perhaps a psychiatrist might argue that Ralph left the door ajar unconsciously because he was hoping that someone would come in and kill Stella in her sleep.

But this we may leave for the psychiatrists to puzzle out among themselves. What is important is the fact that Ralph left the door open.

This made it possible for Maria Raines to walk into the apartment while Stella slept.

Maria was a mess. Her beautiful black hair was tangled and snarled; her clothes looked as though they had been slept in. In a manner of speaking, this was not far from the truth. What sleep Maria had had, she had in her clothes.

Larry and Sally had gone home together. They didn't even tell Maria they were leaving and when she looked around for Larry he had already gone. She had to walk all the way home to their apartment by herself. When she arrived there Larry told her she couldn't live with him anymore.

The rest of what had happened was a large blur in her mind. She wandered all over the Village, her head in a whirl and tears pouring periodically from her eyes and running down her cheeks. She was very tired but there was no one for her to go to, no place for her to sleep. She didn't even have enough money for a room at a cheap hotel.

Finally she managed to find her way onto the subway and collapse into a seat. She couldn't really sleep, but every once in a while her mind would wander and her eyes would close for five or ten or fifteen minutes. It wasn't very satisfactory but it was better than no sleep at all.

After a time she tired of the subway. She got off in the Village and wandered some more. After a good bit of walking she ran into a man with whom she had spent the night once and talked him into buying her some breakfast.

The food stuck in her throat. She couldn't eat at all at first, but she knew it was important for her to eat something and she managed to bolt the food down and keep it down.

When her feet led her to 69 Barrow Street she hesitated outside in the vestibule. She didn't want to ring Stella's bell. She waited instead until somebody else left the building and caught the door before it slammed shut. Then, once inside, she was relieved to find Stella's door ajar.

She entered the apartment. The sight of it sent her head reeling as she remembered what a bad girl she had been the night before. She was always such a bad little girl, such a horrid child. That was why Larry had thrown her out, and that was why nobody ever loved her, not even her own mother. Why, she must have been bad all her life. Why else would her mother hate her so much?

She paused at the door of Stella's bedroom. She knew how bad it was to walk into someone's bedroom without knocking. Why, she could remember so very clearly the time she was a very little girl and she walked into her mother's bedroom without knocking and her mother was with her father and they were . . .

Well, at the time she hadn't the slightest idea what they were doing. But she was being very bad and her mother punished her for that. She could remember it all very clearly, every bit of it.

But what if she knocked and Stella was sleeping? Then Stella would be very angry with her, and she didn't want that to happen.

She compromised with herself by knocking three times, very gently so as not to disturb Stella if she was asleep. There was no answer, so she turned the doorknob carefully and pushed the door open and walked in.

Stella was asleep.

Maria looked down at her, looked at her superb naked body and her full rich mouth. She remembered the first time, with all the men taking her and then with Stella holding her and petting her like a little puppy dog and telling her that everything would be all right.

She loved Stella.

And at the same time she hated Stella.

It was all very confusing.

Moments after Ralph knocked, the door opened and Susan motioned for him to come into the room. He followed her inside and glanced around her apartment, mentally contrasting the quiet nearness of it with the filth and disorder of the apartment he had just left. The furniture in Susan's apartment was all freshly dusted and nothing was out of place.

As an artist, Ralph naturally was convinced that an apartment, like clothing and grooming, reflected a certain facet of a person's personality. The impression he got walking into Susan's living room tended to reinforce this opinion.

So did Susan.

She had obviously been up for only a short while. Her breakfast dishes were still on the table in the kitchenette and the coffee cup was only half empty. But she was already wide awake, neatly dressed and perfectly self-possessed. Her eyes were shining and her hair was combed.

"I'm glad to see you," she said, helping him set up his easel and unload the rest of his equipment.

"For a while I thought you weren't coming," she continued. "You had me worried."

"I was up late last night. Just got up."

"Well, I'm glad you came. You know, I've been pretty excited since yesterday."

"About what?"

"About getting my picture done."

"Oh, it's hardly anything to get excited about."

She sat down at the dinner table and he took a seat across from her. "I think it might be," she said. "You've got to remember that this is something completely new to me. I'll probably do everything all wrong."

"Don't worry about it."

"Will you let me know when I goof?"

"I'll probably yell at you."

"I wish you would," she said, grinning. "I can take it, and I want to know what I'm doing wrong."

She finished her coffee and carried her dishes to the sink.

Automatically he joined her and picked up a dish towel, drying the dishes as she washed them.

"Let's get started," she said as soon as the dishes were all put away in the cabinet. "I'm ready whenever you are."

"Fine."

"How do you want me to pose?"

"First you better pick out some clothes that you like. This may take a lot of sittings and it's easy to get tired of putting on the same clothing all the time."

She thought for a minute. "Would you rather I posed nude?"

"Whatever you want."

"Tell me," she persisted.

"Well," he said, "I'd rather do you nude. Otherwise the clothes sort of get in the way. The artist spends as much time getting the folds right in a skirt as he does on the person he's painting. It's a pain in the neck.

"Besides," he added, "I've always been able to get more of the subject across with nudes. But it's entirely up to you, Susan."

"I'm not embarrassed," she said. "And it might be fun, in a way."

She disappeared into the bedroom. When she returned a few moments later he had to catch his breath. She was stark naked—and she was far and away the most attractive woman he had ever seen in his life.

It took him a moment to realize that he was staring at her, and as soon as he realized it he flushed. "I'm sorry," he stammered. "I didn't mean to stare."

She didn't say anything.

"You're almost unbelievably beautiful," he said. "I couldn't help myself. It'll be a pleasure to paint you."

"Thank you."

Suddenly he was all business. He moved the easy chair about twelve feet from the window and set up the easel midway between chair and window. He raised the shade all the way and flung the window open.

"Good light," he said.

"Do you want me to sit in the chair?"

He nodded. "For one thing, I don't want to give you a difficult pose. It's hard enough to remain in a comfortable position for a long stretch and there's no sense looking for trouble."

"What's the other thing?"

He looked at her.

"You said for one thing. What's the other?"

"Oh." He walked to the chair and showed her how to sit in it, facing the easel head-on with both feet on the floor and her legs spread slightly. He had her fold her hands and rest them over her groin.

"This is the other thing," he explained. "This pose should be perfect for you."

"How do you mean?"

"A pose is very important, Susan. It has a lot to do with the effect that the artist is trying to capture. Keep your back straight—that's right. You see, whatever the painter is trying to get across in a portrait, that effect is either enhanced or destroyed by the way he poses his subject."

"What effect are you trying to put across?"

He hesitated. "It's an emotional thing, of course. It's hard to translate it into a word."

"Can you give me some idea?"

"Well—innocence."

She smiled. "Really?"

He nodded.

"Is that how I impress you?"

"Yes," he said. "Sort of an inner innocence, if you know what I mean. As if nothing has ever really touched you. A knowing innocence, but an innocence nevertheless."

"Wow," she said. "I feel as though I've taken off my skin as well as my clothes."

He grinned. "That's perfect," he said. "Hold that pose. And don't smile like that—I don't want to make you look *too* knowing."

Maria walked to Stella's side. Hesitantly she reached out with one hand and touched Stella on the shoulder. Then she jerked her hand away, fearing that she had done something wrong.

Stella woke up at once.

For a moment she stared at Maria without recognizing her. Then she smiled.

"Oh," she said. "It's you."

Maria nodded.

"What are you doing here?"

"Larry threw me out," she said. "I was a bad girl and he threw me out."

"What did you do that was so bad?"

"I don't know."

Stella considered. "Well, where are you going to live now?"

"I don't know."

"Do you have any money?"

The girl shook her head.

"How about your family?"

"They would never let me come home," Maria stated solemnly. "I'm a bad girl. My mother would never let me come home."

"I see."

"And I don't have any place to go."

Stella closed her eyes for a second, thinking. "There's a vacant room in this building," she said. "It's just a room with no place to cook, just a single room. Would you like to live in it?"

"I would like that," Maria said.

"It's not very big."

"That doesn't matter."

"And you'll have to do whatever I tell you to do," Stella went on. "I'll be paying your rent and buying your meals, so you'll have to obey me all the time."

Maria nodded.

"Will you do that?"

Maria nodded again.

"You'll have to try to be a good girl."

"I'll try."

"And when you're bad I'll punish you."

"I'm very bad," Maria said. "All the time I'm bad. I'm a bad little girl."

"If you're bad I'll punish you."

"That's what my mother said," Maria said dreamily. "She always punished me when I was bad."

"How?"

"She spanked me. She spanked me hard."

"I see," Stella said.

"My Mummy is very strong," Maria said. "She spanks hard."

"Sometimes that's the best thing in the world for a bad little girl."

Maria nodded, agreeing.

"Have you been bad lately?"

"Yes," Maria said. "I was very bad last night. I was horrid."

"Do you think I ought to give you a spanking?"

Maria nodded again.

"Then take off all your clothes." Without a word Maria began to strip. She unbuttoned her blouse and removed it. She had left her bra at the apartment the night before, and Stella's eyes fastened on the soft, beautifully formed breasts. Then she unzipped her skirt and stepped out of it. She pulled down her panties and kicked off her shoes.

"Come here," Stella ordered. The girl obeyed.

Stella sat up in bed with her legs out in front of her. She, too, was nude.

"I want you to lie across my knees," Stella said. "And then you will get your punishment."

The girl did as she was told. "Can I call you Mummy?" she demanded suddenly.

"Of course," Stella said. "I'm your Mummy and you're my bad little girl."

"That's right," Maria said. "That's right, Mummy."

Stella breathed quickly. Then she began to rain blows on the beautiful girl's soft little backside, slapping with the palms of her hands, using first one hand and then the other. At first the spanking was fairly soft, but as she went on she began to slap harder and harder until she was putting all the force of her powerful arms into the blows.

"That hurts, Mummy!"

"It's supposed to hurt," Stella explained. "It's your punishment."

The girl accepted the explanation.

At last, when the little girl began to cry softly and steadily, Stella decided that she had had enough. Gently she rolled Maria over onto her back and stretched out beside her.

"It hurts," Maria whimpered. "You hurt me, Mummy."

"My poor little girl," Stella murmured. She lowered her lips to Maria's and kissed her gently on the mouth. Then she pecked softly at her cheek.

"I love you, Mummy."

Unable to restrain herself any longer, Stella let out a little sob of passion and took the girl in her arms.

Chapter 6

The days passed.

Times goes by everywhere, and in this case Greenwich Village is not an exception. By day the sun beat down hot and bright between the buildings and at night the buildings held the heat in close. It was summer in New York, and like every summer in New York it was thoroughly unbearable.

But Ralph didn't find the heat too objectionable. He was settling down into what was for him a relatively comfortable routine. Every afternoon he mounted the stairs to Susan's apartment and worked on the portrait. The work went slowly; Susan's beauty had an elusive quality about it which was difficult to capture in oils. Every brushstroke was important and every shade lighter or darker made a tangible difference.

He left his painting supplies in Susan's room each day when he finished his work. The partially completed canvas he covered with a white cloth, instructing the girl not to remove it to look at the painting.

"I want you to see it all at once," he told her. "No sneak previews."

She teased him, anxious for a look. But he was adamant.

And, as the days passed, Stella demanded less and less of his time. With Maria established permanently in a tiny room on the second floor Stella had found a ready and willing outlet for her sexual abnormalities, and the two women were together almost constantly.

More than once that week Stella had given him Maria's key and told him to leave them alone for the evening.

Ralph was glad to be left alone. For the first time in a long time he was completely absorbed in his work, wrapped up in it so deeply that his mind was on the painting even when he was far from Susan's room, even when he was lying in bed and ready for sleep. After only a few days with the girl he could have painted her portrait from memory, so firmly was her appearance fixed in his mind. Every shadow and line, every perfect detail of her perfect head and body was imprinted upon his memory.

But the thought of finishing the picture alone was a thought that he couldn't take seriously for a moment. He enjoyed Susan's company much too much to give up a second of it. For the first time in his life he found himself able to talk to a girl, to tell her all the things that were on his mind and to listen to everything she had to tell him. He talked to her about his childhood, about the small town in Ohio and the small local college, about his hitch in the army and the void that followed it.

He told her about Stella—about the cruel and twisted woman he lived with. And he told her all these things without shame or fear, knowing that she was listening sympathetically and accepting all that he told her.

For the first several days he did the bulk of the talking. She would be sitting on the chair in the pose he had selected, both feet on the floor a foot or so apart, her small hands folded over her pubic area, her back straight and her mouth unsmiling. She would sit and listen, her face never changing expression while he went over his life in detail.

Then, after a while, she began to talk. She too started with her childhood and moved on, through the years in school to the years after school. One afternoon with no show of embarrassment she explained to him that she was a lesbian. Inwardly he flinched but he made no outward show of surprise or irritation. After all, he had been almost certain of it already.

She told him about the women she had been with, about the fear of men that overwhelmed her. And even as she told him these things, even as she bared her soul and confessed her secret, something happened to him.

Something that had been happening all along. Something that he had refused to see coming, but something that he was quite unable to prevent.

He fell in love with her.

That evening he left the building as soon as he finished the day's painting. He walked out the door without even pausing at his own apartment, and he walked west on Barrow Street toward the Hudson River.

He walked slowly.

The love he felt for Susan was something new and different, something totally out of the ordinary and totally removed from emotions he had felt in the past. It was a fresh, vibrant feeling, and it was all the more beautiful for the absolute hopelessness of it all.

Ralph had been in love before. In a way he had even been in love with Stella, although he felt less and less for her every day. But all his previous affairs had begun with a strong physical attraction that had sexual gratification as their prime objective. After that they occasionally ripened into something more, something approaching love if not love itself.

This was different.

He never laid a hand on Susan. From the moment he met her he was conscious of the striking beauty of the girl, but somehow he had never thought of her as a woman to take to bed, a woman to make a pass at. Instead she represented friendship to him—friendship in the classic sense, coupled with a deep exchange of ideas and a sharing of secrets. That in itself was a very valuable and rewarding sort of thing, and the ensuing relationship had turned out to be a wonderful one.

But now—

Now he was in love with her.

What did it mean? How in the world could he be in love with a girl whom he would never be able to make love to? He not only could never marry her, but he could never take her in his arms, never kiss her or touch her. What kind of love was this?

He kept walking, laughing bitterly to himself. It was a typical Ralph Lambert play, he decided. Only a guy like him could do a scatterbrained, useless thing like this. Only a guy like him could fall in love with a lesbian and get all hung up about it.

What in the world would happen? She hadn't had any lovers since she had moved to Barrow Street, but he knew that in time she would have to. Then what would he do? Maybe he'd be jealous of the other girl. That would be one for the books, wouldn't it? Ralph Lambert jealous of a dyke. Pretty funny, huh? Yeah. A riot.

Fantasies flooded his mind, fantasies of possible courses of action. He knew that she had never been with a man, and he guessed that her traumatic fear might stem as much from ignorance of sex as anything else. He remembered reading that blind, ignorant fear was a prime cause of what one author termed "the homosexual neurosis"—that a person who was afraid of sex was less likely to fear someone of the same sex than someone of the opposite sex. To Susan another woman might represent the Known, something she was familiar with because it was similar to herself. A man, on the other hand, was the Unknown—and she had to fear him more because the Unknown was so much more terrifying.

He fancied himself for a moment as a knight on a white charger coming to rescue her from her homosexuality by showing her that she had nothing to be afraid of. Then the barriers would break down one by one until she came to him and he held her in his arms, held that sweet and beautiful body that he had studied so carefully and reproduced so faithfully.

Then—

Suddenly the hilarious impossibility of the situation struck him full force and a hysterical laugh shrieked forth from his lips. He stood on the sidewalk, unable to stop laughing, and was forced to grab onto a lamppost for support. Other people on the street stared at him as he laughed and laughed over something that was not funny at all.

Finally he caught his breath and started walking again. He

walked all over the west side of the Village, looking for something but not knowing what it was that he was looking for. He kept walking until he found the bar.

It wasn't much. It was a run-down longshoreman's bar down by the docks where the liquor was cheap and the air foul smelling. A jukebox in one corner blared forth with raucous rock-and-roll. A tired prostitute sat at a table in the back, a professional smile on her once-attractive face. A row of tired-looking, husky men drank shots with beer chasers at the long brown bar.

It was a place to drink. That was all he wanted, a place where he could be alone by himself without being entirely alone, a place where he could sit and drink with nobody bothering him.

A place that had neither Stella nor Susan around, a place where the only woman present was a cheap waterfront whore.

He walked into the bar. One stool was vacant and he sat down on it. He ordered a shot of the bar whiskey and a glass of draft beer for a chaser.

The shot was a quarter and the beer was a dime. It was about as cheap as you could get any place in the city.

When he had finished pouring the shot down his throat he knew why it only cost two bits. It was rotgut—cheap moonshine brought in from Kentucky and sold with ease because the cop on the beat knew who was paying him. A steady diet of it would raise hell with the lining of a man's stomach, but it was cheap and it would get a person stoned out of his head as quickly as the stuff that went for six bucks a fifth.

He sipped the beer. It was a little watery but not too bad. He finished it and motioned for the bartender.

This time he ordered a double.

•   •   •

Stella dressed quickly after she finished her shower. Maria had already returned to her room on the second floor, and for some reason Stella felt empty and unfulfilled. She wasn't sure why, but for one reason or another her evening with the little brunette had left her less satisfied than before.

Why? The girl was cooperative enough. Their little game of the bad little girl being punished by her angry mother had gone along nicely for some time now, and each time the punishments themselves had been more extreme and consequently more exciting to Stella. At one time or other she had struck every surface of Maria's shapely body with harsh blows until the little girl was black and blue all over. She had devised many different exotic methods for causing Maria to sob and quiver with pain, each method more stimulating to both of them than the last.

Maria never called her by name any more. She referred to her always as Mummy and demanded punishment constantly. Idly Stella wondered what event deep in Maria's childhood had brought on this unnatural craving for punishment and pain. What had the girl done?

It didn't matter. What mattered right now, Stella decided, was finding some way to calm herself down. Whatever the reason, Maria had been unable to still her hunger and she felt a desperate need for something more, something that would enable her to relax. Mentally she went over the men and women that she could call up for an evening's diversion.

There were none she could think of that interested her in the least.

Where was Ralph? She had been seeing less and less of him lately, but what was even more aggravating was the fact that he seemed to be slipping away from her. She needed Ralph. She needed someone permanent, someone she could hold onto.

Was there something between him and the little dyke who was posing for him? It didn't seem likely. If any girl had impressed her as an obvious lesbian, Susan Rivers had. But Ralph was obviously interested in the girl—and he was spending plenty of time with her.

Christ, maybe she had hit the nail on the head that time when the two of them had breakfast together! Suppose Ralph had fallen for the girl. It was just the sort of bonehead maneuver the guy was capable of, and with her posing for him every day it was more than possible.

If that was the case—

She smiled, her lips curling into a vicious grin. If that was the case her own course of action was clear. She could utterly crush Ralph and enjoy herself at the same time. It would all be quite perfect.

She left the apartment and closed the door behind her. Then, very deliberately she climbed the stairs to the fourth floor. She found Susan Rivers' door and knocked gently on it.

She waited impatiently, shifting her weight from foot to foot until the door opened.

Susan was standing there. She was dressed in a blue kimono. Her feet were bare.

Stella let her eyes run impudently from Susan's face all the way to her bare feet and back again. Then a smile appeared on her face.

"My name is Stella James," she said slowly. "Could I come inside for a minute?"

Ralph's fingers closed around the shot glass. He tried to remember how many drinks he had had so far but couldn't. Then he tried to remember how many drinks he had poured down his throat since he stopped bothering with beer chasers.

He couldn't remember that either.

He stared into the liquor. A face swam on top of the liquor. The face had short dark brown hair and no makeup. The face was not smiling. The face was also very beautiful.

The face looked familiar. It was, of course, the face of Susan Rivers. And a very lovely face it was.

He drained the glass and set it down gently on the top of the bar. The face was gone.

The liquor hadn't burned his throat on the way down. That was one of the good things about a drinking bout—after a few drinks the bilge didn't taste vile anymore. As a matter of fact it didn't have any taste whatsoever. It just worked its way down his throat and into his stomach, and the alcohol seeped into his stomach and nothing seemed to matter as much as it did when he was sober.

There was, he reflected, very little point in being sober. When you were sober you could see things quite clearly, much too clearly for your own good. And there was very little point in seeing things clearly. No point, actually. No point at all, not when your name was Ralph Lambert and you lived with a bitch named Stella and loved a lesbian named Susan Rivers. No point at all.

The bartender, whose name happened to be Charlie, came over and looked at Ralph with a puzzled expression on his flat face.

"Ya wanna nudder?" Charlie demanded.

"Ah," Ralph said. "Hello, Charlie."

"Hello."

"You don't mind if I call you Charlie, do you?"

"It's my name."

"Some people might mind."

"Live a little," Charlie suggested. "Call me anything you damn please."

"In that case I'll have another."

"Another double?"

Ralph nodded drunkenly.

"You drink like a goddamn fish," Charlie said.

"That's nothing. I swim like an alcoholic."

"Huh?"

"I drink like a fish and swim like a drunk."

"Oh," said Charlie. "I get it. Better it should be the other way around."

Ralph nodded.

"You do this often? Not that it's any of my business. I just wondered."

"Only when I fall in love with a lesbian."

"Huh?"

"A lesbian," Ralph explained, waving one hand at no one in particular. "I fell in love with a lesbian."

"That's a female fairy?"

"Precisely."

"Jeez," Charlie said. "And you're really in love with the broad?"

"Precisely."

"Ain't it a bitch. What are you gonna do?"

"I'm going to have another drink."

"That sounds like a wise move," Charlie said. "I mean what the hell else can you do?"

"Precisely."

"Jeez," Charlie repeated. "A lesbian."

Ralph nodded.

"She good-looking?"

"She's the most beautiful woman in the world."

"You getting anything?"

"Not a thing."

Charlie poured a double shot of the bar whiskey and pushed it across to Ralph. "Live a little," he said. "This one's on the house. This don't happen every day."

Ralph gulped the drink. "I should hope not," he said. "It would kill me."

Susan sat alone in her room. Stella had just left, a haunting smile on her lips and a provocative swing to her hips as she walked out of the room.

Susan was afraid again.

She stood up and began pacing the floor, up and down, back and forth. Her breath came in quick, short gasps. She walked from the living room to the bathroom to the kitchen, looking vaguely for something but unsure what it was that she was looking for.

Fear.

It seemed as though she was going to live her entire life immersed in a sea of fear. There was no getting away from it. There was nothing she could do, no way out that was open to her.

She had been afraid of Stella from the first time they met on the stoop. That was bad enough, but with the passage of time her fear had begun to fade away. Even Ralph's descriptions of Stella, his explanation of the type of woman she was—even this had not truly shaken her.

But one conversation with Stella James had her shaking. She could hardly think straight anymore.

The funny thing was that Stella hadn't actually *done* anything. She simply came in and sat down and started an extremely innocent conversation about how she had seen Susan from time to time and how she wanted to meet her. That was all.

It was what went unsaid that set the girl on edge. Stella made it obvious that she was ready and willing to play, that she was more than game for a hot little dose of lesbian love. She didn't have to say anything to get her point across. It was obvious in every act, every word, every gesture and every glance.

No, it was more than that. It would be bad enough if she was merely offering herself. Then Susan would still have the prerogative of refusing the offer, and while that would be difficult it would be her choice, her right to choose between sex and solitude. But instead Stella was saying *I'm going to have you and you can't stop me.*

And this was very frightening. More than frightening.

Terrifying.

Because she didn't want sex with Stella. Well, she had to admit to herself that this wasn't entirely true. In one way, a purely physical way, she wanted sex with Stella desperately. She had been alone for too long and her body was beginning to crave a woman's hands on it, her mouth to hunger for a woman's lips pressing against them. But this was a physical hunger and nothing more.

Both intellectually and emotionally she wanted only to be left alone. While the idea of a woman making love to her was less repelling by far than that of a man doing the same things, she knew that it was necessary for her to live a celibate life for the time being, if only so that she could get her bearings and determine precisely what course she was going to follow in the future. This was a hard thing to do, but it was a vital thing also.

Ralph was good for her. He was never on the make, never hungry or grasping. And he was always there, always ready to talk or to listen to her, always sharing a part of himself with her. There was absolutely nothing she wouldn't be willing to tell him, no secret she wouldn't reveal to him. He seemed to understand virtually everything, or at least to accept whatever he didn't understand.

She wasn't afraid of Ralph. And because she could be with him and open herself up to him she was beginning to relax, beginning to calm down a little inside. She could even feel that her life was becoming somehow healthier and more meaningful.

And then Stella had to walk into her life.

Well, right now there was nothing she could do. She had to wait for things to straighten themselves out in whatever fashion they chose. Tomorrow she could tell Ralph what had happened. Tomorrow everything would be easier because she would have someone to confide in.

Why, Ralph was almost like a psychotherapist for her! He

made her feel so much better. Now, if only Stella would leave her alone . . .

Resolutely she shook her head and walked to the side of her bed. She slipped out of the blue kimono and crawled into bed. She lay on her back for a long time, her eyes staring blankly at the ceiling.

She couldn't stop thinking of Stella.

And, inevitably, her own hands began their gentle course, stroking her breasts and then her stomach, moving downward to her very private and secret place. She touched herself and thought of Stella as she had done before, stroking herself and whispering to herself, thinking of strange and obscene delights.

Just as she had done before.

Only this time she was ashamed of herself.

Ralph floated home.

That wasn't exactly how it happened, but that's how it seemed at the time. He bid Charlie a cheerful goodbye and floated out of the bar. Then he floated into the taxi that Charlie had insisted upon calling for home. Then the taxi floated around for a while until it came to rest in front of 69 Barrow Street. He paid the driver, tipped him two dollars, and floated up the walk to the stoop.

The driver, who hadn't had a two-dollar tip since V-J day, stared long and thoughtfully after Ralph. Then, shaking his head and smiling gently to himself, he started the cab up again and drove off.

Ralph had an enormous amount of difficulty fitting the

key into the lock. He managed it, however, and when the door opened he felt enormously proud of himself. Then he floated down the hallway to his apartment and played games again, trying to get the other key in the lock.

He managed that also and opened the door, feeling more proud of himself than ever. He floated into the room.

Stella was in the bedroom. Surprisingly enough she was alone.

"Hello," he said. "Do you mind if I call you Charlie?"

She just looked at him.

He sat down on the edge of the bed. "Oh," he said. "I thought you were a bartender."

He stood up again and got undressed and ready for bed. Then he sat down again on the edge of the bed and smiled drunkenly at Stella.

Stella said, "I'm going to sleep with your girlfriend."

He shook his head. He figured he must be hearing things, so he waited for her to go on.

"I went up to see her tonight," Stella said. "We had a pleasant chat. She's quite lovely."

"No," he said. He wanted to say more but he couldn't remember just what it was that he wanted to say.

"Yes, Ralph. What's the matter?"

"Don't."

"Why not?" Her smile taunted him.

"Just don't."

"But you'll have to tell me why not. I can't just accept things on your say-so."

"Because she doesn't want you."

"Are you sure?"

He stared at her.

"Don't be too sure," Stella was saying. "Don't be too certain about anything."

"Leave her alone."

"Why?"

He was silent.

"Are you in love with her, Ralph?"

He turned away from her.

"Are you?"

He didn't answer.

"Tell me, Ralph."

"Yes," he said, finally. "I'm in love with her."

"In that case," Stella said, "I'll be sure to let you watch." And she began to laugh hysterically.

He turned to her again. Something flared in him all at once and he couldn't hold back the hate and fury that had been building within him. He grabbed her by one arm and hauled her out of bed, sinking one fist into her stomach.

She folded up like an accordion. Then she began to laugh again through clenched teeth.

"Damn you!" he exploded. He hit her again and again, ringing blows with his open hand that landed on her face and breasts.

But he couldn't still her laughter.

Then, at last, he made love to her. Making love is perhaps the wrong term; what he made was hate. He took her with fury burning through his bloodstream, forcing her back down on the bed and pummeling her with his fists, then taking her cruelly and viciously, hurting her as much as he possibly could.

As soon as he had finished with her he rolled away from her and his head swam. He closed his eyes.

Then, mercifully, the liquor and sex combined and he was unconscious.

CHAPTER 7

He woke up slowly, weakly. First, with his eyes still clenched shut and his frame motionless, consciousness began to return to Ralph. For a long moment he remained in one position without moving his eyelids at all.

When he finally opened his eyes the light hurt them and he shut them again quickly. He tried to yawn and stretch and his muscles ached dully in the process. He breathed heavily and turned over onto his back.

He felt like hell.

He opened his eyes a second time and this time they stayed open. Haltingly he pulled himself to his feet. A wave of dizziness almost knocked him to the floor and he had to clutch the side of the bed for support. He sat down again on the side of the bed with his feet on the floor and stared blindly at the wall.

His mouth was parched, his throat bone-dry. There was a sick, queasy feeling in the pit of his stomach that was spreading quietly throughout his system. His head felt too large and bulky for his neck to support it. His arms, when he reached for his shoes, didn't seem to work as well as they had in the past.

He stood up again. The dizziness slugged him in the teeth again but this time he was able to master it and stay on his feet.

By the elaborate process of putting one foot in front of the other he managed to reach the bathroom and step under the shower.

The shower helped. It didn't do the trick single-handed, of course, and when he finally finished his turn under first the hot spray and then the cold spray and stepped out of the tub again, he felt a good deal better but a long ways from human. The dizziness was still present in a smaller dose and his thirst was unchanged.

He drank glass after glass of cold water, not even pausing to count them. He filled the plastic glass and poured it down his throat again and again in a heroic attempt to fill his stomach with water. Then he took his toothbrush and removed the fuzzy woolen sweaters that seemed to be shrouding his teeth.

He looked in the mirror and shuddered. His eyes were red-rimmed and bloodshot. There was a gash on his cheek where he had evidently managed to cut himself during the night. And his face, in one way or another, had aged a good ten years in the one night. The lines in his forehead and around his nose and mouth had deepened perceptibly. He wondered how much of this was a temporary effect of drunkenness and how much was a permanent change.

Back in the bedroom he dressed slowly and methodically, wondering but not caring where Stella had gone, wondering but not caring how he himself would spend the day, wondering about a great many things but caring about very little of anything. He put on a blue sport shirt and a pair of khaki pants, tied his tennis shoes too tight and had to re-tie them, and at last walked out of the bedroom, out of the apartment, down the hallway and out of the building into the cool air of the morning.

It was a beautiful morning—clear without being too hot yet,

the air fresh and the sky a deep, rich shade of blue. Somehow this only made everything a little worse. If it were drizzling and freezing and otherwise vile it would be more in keeping with the way he felt.

Well, he said to himself, *you really tied one on, you simple bastard.* Talking to himself helped in some way or other and he felt a little bit better for it. His step quickened as he walked to the restaurant for breakfast, the same one where he and Susan had had their first conversation over breakfast.

When he arrived at the restaurant he sat alone in the same booth that he and Susan had occupied before. He ordered scrambled eggs, orange juice, toast and coffee. This, as it turned out, was somewhat on the optimistic side. The coffee was helpful and he was able to get the orange juice and toast down, but no matter how hard he worked at it he couldn't bring himself to eat the eggs. After a while he gave up and glared at them balefully.

Where did he go from here?

It was, he admitted, a good question. A delightfully profound question. He only wished he knew the answer.

He gulped down what coffee was left in his cup and beckoned to the counterman for a refill. The counterman took his cup and filled it up again and Ralph looked down into the coffee, remembering the way he had stared into the shot of liquor the night before to see Susan's face floating upon the liquid.

He couldn't see her face in the cup of coffee. But when he closed his eyes for a brief second, every detail of her face and body flooded his brain and his head began to throb from the vision. He lit a cigarette, which didn't taste good at all, to go with the coffee which tasted like turpentine.

What was he going to do?

Or, to start with, what did he know about the whole thing?

He knew Susan was a lesbian. This didn't require much in the way of perception on his part since she had taken care to inform him of the fact. He knew that he was in love with her, and that the love he felt for her was a very genuine and wholehearted emotion. He also knew—and again it didn't take any genius to figure it out—that as a lesbian Susan didn't have much use for him as a lover.

Which made the whole thing look pretty hopeless.

But he couldn't help engaging in a bit of wishful thinking. Perhaps Susan's lesbianism wasn't anything organic. Perhaps it was her mind rather than her glands which had made her the way she was, her fear of men which had forced her to accept the caresses of women. Deep in his own mind was the notion that he ought to be able to bring Susan out of her shell. If he could convince her that he loved her and that his love wasn't something to be afraid of, there was no reason why she couldn't learn to return his love.

And for once in his life, love was the important thing. Susan was the most thoroughly desirable woman he had ever met, but a sexual relationship with her was something he could do without as long as he had to. He saw in her something far more valuable than a bedmate, far more important than a partner in sex games. A woman like Susan could add a whole new dimension to his life. With her at his side he could get rid of his involvement with Stella once and for all and get back on the road to respectability. The Villagers could talk all they wanted about freedom, but he was convinced that true freedom meant more than the right to wear sloppy clothes and go without brushing your teeth and sleep with everybody who came along.

Freedom meant being free to *do* things. Freedom, or at least the sort of freedom he wanted for himself, meant the freedom to love one person and one person alone, to work toward a goal and to live a life that meant something. And, with Susan, he might be able to achieve this sort of freedom.

It was a cinch he wouldn't make it without her.

God, why was he such a weakling? The thought nagged at him that another stronger man might have a better chance with Susan. But he couldn't even get up the guts to break away from Stella by himself. How in hell could he save Susan when he couldn't even save himself?

Disgusted with himself, he paid the check and left a tip on the table. He lit another cigarette and smoked as he walked slowly back to his apartment. He waited in the vestibule, seeing Stella and Maria in the hallway by the apartment door. After they were inside the apartment he opened the door and walked to the staircase and up the stairs to the fourth floor.

Susan didn't answer his knock. He tried the door; it was open. Inside on the coffee table there was a note for him explaining that she had to get some work done at the ceramics shop but that she would be back fairly soon and he could wait for her. He sat down in the chair where she always posed and waited.

He recognized her steps on the stairway less than an hour later and had the door open for her when she came in. She had a smile on her face and her eyes were bright.

"Hi," she said.

"How did the work go?"

"Very well. The design I'm working on is very tricky, and the first three times I tried it the pot fell. But this time I think it's going to hold up."

They went on talking while she removed her clothing. For the first time she undressed in front of him and he thought to himself that she *couldn't* be a lesbian, that if she was there was still a chance for him, that she was so natural about everything she did that she could learn to be natural about sex as well. He looked at her, marveling how each time he saw her body it was like seeing it for the first time, how each time he talked with her he fell in love with her all over again.

She sat down in the chair without being told and assumed the pose automatically. He removed the rag that covered the painting and began mixing paint on his palette.

Then he looked at her and stopped what he was doing. He looked long and hard at her, first at her body for only a second and then very carefully at her face.

"What's the matter?"

He started to tell her that nothing was the matter, that he was merely trying to determine how to get the right color for her eyes. But the words didn't come out.

"Ralph?"

He didn't recognize his own voice when he said, "I love you."

She looked at him, still not certain what he was talking about. She waited for him to explain.

And, because he loved her, because he could never hold anything back from her, he told her. He told her all of it, from the beginning to the end, from Alpha to Omega. He didn't omit a thing.

His voice never changed expression while he spoke. His eyes never wavered from hers. The words poured out of him one after the other and she listened in absolute unprotesting silence until he was finished.

When he stopped talking there was silence that was louder than words. They looked at each other; then her gaze dropped to her feet.

A small voice said: "It can't happen, Ralph."

He waited for her to say more.

"I wish this hadn't happened," she went on. "I should have known it was too good to be true, the kind of thing we had. We became so close that I should have seen this coming. I guess I didn't because I didn't want to."

He didn't say anything.

"Don't love me, Ralph."

"I can't help it."

"No, of course not. I suppose you've been fighting the whole affair too. But I can't help wishing I could just take your love and turn it off."

"Like a faucet?"

"Like a faucet. But I guess things don't work out that way."

"Not love."

"Love." She spoke the word not bitterly or sarcastically but in a tone totally devoid of expression as if she was trying the word out on her tongue to see how it sounded coming from her lips.

"Love," she repeated.

He hesitated. Then he said, "Susan, don't you feel anything for me?"

"Of course I do."

"Tell me what you feel."

She considered for a moment, trying to get the words in the right order. "It's hard to explain, Ralph. I . . . well, I like you very much, but that doesn't describe it. I feel very close to you and I care an awful lot about you and I like to be near you and—"

She broke off.

He lit another cigarette. He took one puff of it and expelled the smoke in a rush. Then he watched the cigarette as it rested between his fingers, watching the smoke curl toward the ceiling.

"I think I'm in love with you, Ralph."

His heart sang. But there was something in her tone that made him wait for her to finish.

She said, "But it's not the same kind of love, Ralph. I love you and I want to be near you. And I want to talk to you and I want you to talk to me and . . . and I suppose in a selfish way I want you to love me. It's selfish of me and not right at all but it's something I can't help. I love you, Ralph. I must have known it unconsciously all along; when you told me how you felt I couldn't dodge it any more. I'm in love with you.

"But . . . but I don't want to make love with you or to have you kiss me or touch me or anything. I don't want that, and, I mean—"

She broke off again. He could see tears welling up in the corners of her brown eyes and he sensed the tenseness of her facial muscles as she struggled to keep the tears from flowing down her face.

"Ralph, do you see what I mean?"

He nodded.

"Then you see that it could never work out. Nothing could work out. I love you—but you could never touch me. Our love could never get off the ground."

He started to say something but stopped.

"It's no use, Ralph."

"Susan—"

"Go ahead."

"Susan, we can give it a chance. I've already told you that sex isn't the main thing. It can wait, darling. We can wait with it until you're ready. And I think you will be ready in time, ready to love me as fully as any woman ever loved any man. But it will take time, probably a great deal of time. There are a whole lot of fears and worries that have to go first.

"I'm willing to wait, Susan."

He could hear the wind outside the window. He could hear the clock ticking in the other room. He could hear Susan breathing very quickly and shallowly.

She said, "I'm afraid."

"There's nothing to be afraid of."

"It's not fair, Ralph. It's not fair to you."

"I'm not complaining."

She thought for a moment.

"No," she said, positively, "I can't ask anything like that of you. It's just not fair."

"You're not asking me, darling. I'm asking you."

"You know what I mean. It's too much to expect of any man. Why, it's possible that I would never be able to love you in a sexual way. We would go on forever and after a little while we'd be making each other miserable. You'd hate me, Ralph."

"I couldn't possibly hate you. No matter what happened, no matter what you did or didn't do."

"That's not true. You'd keep wanting me and I wouldn't want you and . . . and before very long we'd be at each other's throat constantly. It wouldn't be good that way, Ralph."

"You've got to give it a chance."

"A chance?"

He nodded. "You can't drop things like this. We have to know, darling. This is too important to risk losing it so easily."

They fell silent. Outside the wind was blowing faster and the sky was getting darker with clouds obscuring the face of the sun. The air grew cooler.

"Ralph."

He looked at her.

"Come here."

He walked to her side. He looked at her, his eyes studying the brown hair, the well-formed breasts, the slender waist. Her hands were still unconsciously arranged over her groin in the pose they had been using, and he wondered if it indicated anything more than that she hadn't thought to move them. Perhaps, unconsciously, she was protecting herself, keeping her body safe from him by the gesture.

"Kiss me, Ralph."

He didn't question her. He knelt beside her, his head swimming at being so close to her naked form. He brought his face close to hers and touched her lips with his, gently, tenderly.

The kiss lasted only an instant. Then he drew away and smiled hesitantly at her.

"Kiss me the way . . . the way a man kisses a woman that he's in love with."

He didn't need encouragement. He kissed her the way he had wanted to kiss her in the first place, the way he had wanted to kiss her for days now. His lips pressed down upon hers and his arms locked around her, pulling them together. He kneeled on the chair and leaned his body against hers. His lips forced hers apart and his tongue slipped into her mouth, seeking, caressing her mouth and tongue.

The kiss took a long time. Before it ended he felt her go limp and he was unsure whether the limpness was a sign of response or rejection.

He found out.

When they broke apart she fell back in the chair and he sat down heavily on the floor at her feet. He looked up into her eyes and she looked down at him and their eyes locked.

At first her face was expressionless. Then her shoulders sank and her eyes flooded over with the tears she had been holding back so long.

And he knew, and the knowledge hit him in the head like a poleax.

"I'm sorry," she said.

"There's nothing to be sorry about."

"Yes, there is."

"Nothing that's your fault."

"It's not your fault either."

He didn't say anything. There didn't seem to be anything to say. Slowly he pulled himself to a standing position and looked down at her once again, trying with his eyes to delve into the girl, to understand precisely what made her tick and what was keeping her from loving him in the same way that he loved her.

She smiled sadly.

"You didn't mind the first time I kissed you."

"It was a different sort of a kiss," she said. "It was almost a . . . a friendly kiss, Ralph. Not passionate in the least."

"But the second time?"

She shivered.

"What . . . bothered you?"

She leaned back in the chair and let her eyes close. In that position her face looked very relaxed and she seemed to be at peace with the world and entirely at ease. But when she spoke her voice came out in a strangled fashion and the effect of relaxation was shattered.

"I felt as though . . . as though you were raping me, Ralph. It's hard for me to explain it exactly. You were kissing me and your tongue was in my mouth and I felt as though . . . as though I was being—"

"Yes?"

"—well, penetrated. I just couldn't stand it and I was getting more and more frightened and generally shook up until you stopped."

He thought for a minute. "When . . . when you kiss a woman, is that how you kiss?"

"More or less."

"And have women kissed you like that?"

"Uh-huh."

"Then—"

"There's a difference, Ralph. Not just in the mechanics of the kiss. Ralph, I think I'm just a lesbian and there's nothing anybody can do about it."

"Don't say that!"

"I'm afraid it's the truth. I'm afraid the reason I'm afraid of you is simply that you're a man and I'm a freak who only enjoys sex with women. I guess that's all there is to it, Ralph."

"I can't believe that. There's too much between us for it to be just that."

"But—"

"It'll take time," he said doggedly. "It'll take a hell of a lot of time, more time than I thought it would at first. But we'll manage. We love each other."

"Yes," she said. "We love each other."

They talked for a minute or two more; then Ralph covered the canvas once again and left. He was in no mood to do any more painting for the rest of the day and he knew better than to push himself once he hit a real snag. It was too easy to foul yourself up completely that way and ruin a painting that was good until then.

He walked down the stairs again, his feet heavy on the steps. He passed the closed door of his own apartment and hurried out to the street. He wanted to keep moving, to go where nobody knew him and to do pretty much of nothing.

He was in no mood for people—not for Susan or Stella certainly, not for the moment. The IRT subway let him off at Times Square and he deliberated between getting quietly bombed out of his head or trying to lose himself in a cheap movie. The movie won—drinking didn't sound too attractive with the hangover he had just gone through, and the movie was also a good deal cheaper.

He saw a double feature without seeing it. Afterward he remembered very vaguely that one of the films was something about gangsters and starred either George Raft or Jimmy Cagney, but he couldn't remember for sure which one it was. The other picture was an "Eastern Western"—the saga of Genghis Khan or some such, with people riding around on rabid camels and shooting rifles which, as Ralph remembered, weren't in such wide distribution at the time of Genghis Khan. But he couldn't be sure.

Throughout both movies his eyes stared at the screen while only half seeing it. His mind was elsewhere, wrapped up in the problems he had tried to leave behind him when he walked into the theater. As usual, it didn't work. He found himself remembering the taste of Susan's lips when he kissed her—the first time gently, the second time with a passion that had been too much for her.

The taste of her lips, the clean sweet smell of her naked flesh so close to him, her breasts pressing against his shirtfront. His hands meeting behind her back as he pressed her close. The feel of her bare back under his hands, soft and clean and smooth, slender without being thin. The warm taste inside her mouth, the touch of her tongue.

Sensory impressions flooded his brain as his mind turned time and time to the kiss and the conversation that followed it. The impressions mingled with the love he felt for her and killed whatever interest the two movies might have held for him.

He didn't like movies too much to begin with, generally preferring a paperback book to even a top-notch picture. There was one great thing for both reading and looking at paintings—you could do them on your own time and pace yourself as you pleased. If you were a fast reader you could read quickly; if you felt like it you could slow down. But speeding up a movie or playing a 33-rpm record at 78 didn't work out.

He left the theatre when the second picture ended and found his way to an inexpensive restaurant on 47th Street. He ate a meal without tasting it and smoked a cigarette without even realizing that he had lighted one. Finally he wandered to the Museum of Modern Art on Fifth Avenue and spent several hours studying some of his favorite paintings.

Modigliani had always been his favorite painter—the feeling and warmth in his nudes and portraits of men and women with long necks and narrow heads communicated itself strongly to him. As he stood for a long time in front of the portrait of the Young Girl with Braids he was reminded vaguely of Susan. Both shared the same quality of innocence in the eyes and around the mouth.

He thought about Modigliani and the kind of life the man had led. Sickly as a child, he moved to Paris while in his early twenties and seemed determined to kill himself as quickly as possible. He drank almost constantly; when he wasn't drinking he was smoking opium or hashish or experimenting with still stronger drugs.

The artist's motto had been "Une vie breve mais intense"—a short life but an intense one. That was a perfect description of what he achieved, contracting tuberculosis and dying in his mid-thirties. And then his mistress Jeanne Hebuterne had thrown herself from the balcony of her father's house to join him in death.

He shook his head. Compared to that, his own life seemed almost sane. But he knew that he was walking a tightrope and could fall either way at any moment. If he lost Susan he was afraid to think what would happen to him. He knew for a fact that he would never paint again. He would pack up his paints and brushes and canvases and chuck them in the nearest trashcan. And he would probably start hitting the bottle fairly regularly, drifting deeper and deeper into the life of perversion and depravity that Stella represented.

For a moment he remembered the night before when he had returned to listen to Stella's taunts. He hoped again that Stella would leave Susan alone. Even if he himself couldn't have her, the girl deserved a lot better deal than Stella would hand her.

But what an animal he himself had turned to last night! That's what would happen to him if he lost the girl; he was sure of it, sure that he would react by throwing up everything and striking back the only way he knew how.

At nine o'clock he left the museum and wandered back toward Times Square. He didn't want to go back to Barrow Street, not now. He couldn't face either of the two women who might be waiting for him.

Instead he took a room for the night at a run-down hotel on 47th Street, paying in advance. The room was a rat-trap—a small single bed, about a foot of space on each side of the bed, the bathroom down the hall, the room's window opening out on a brick wall.

But it was a place to sleep, a place to be alone. That was all he wanted for the time being.

CHAPTER 8

Susan stared at the closed door for a long time after he left her. Her mind was a jumble of confused thoughts and half-thoughts, a collection of random whirling notions, a hodgepodge of feelings and lusts and drives and inhibitions all rolled together. She didn't know for sure how she felt or what she wanted.

She stood up and paced the room for a few moments, her trim legs carrying her back and forth from the window to the door. She paused at the window for a moment to see if she could find Ralph but he was already out of sight. Standing by the window, her breasts heaving, she realized all at once that she was naked. She blushed automatically and took a quick step away, wondering whether or not anyone had seen her.

Of course it really didn't matter one way or the other. But everything was turmoilish enough as things stood without her inflaming some poor man outside who happened to be star-gazing. She tossed herself down in the armchair out of sight—but now that the idea had come into her head the idea of sitting around naked made her uncomfortable.

She remembered that time when she and Sharon had discovered a Peeping Tom in the building across the street. The nervy son of a bitch had a pair of binoculars trained on their window and was getting himself a good eyeful. He must have been getting his kicks in style—instead of watching one girl take off her clothes he had the rare opportunity of watching two girls making love.

But after they spotted him and his damned binoculars they ruined his little game forever by lowering the blinds before so much as unzipping a zipper or unbuttoning a button.

She dressed nervously now, her whole mind still reeling in circles. She had been telling Ralph the whole truth, and it was tough for her to tell the truth in a case like this. For that matter it was hard to be sure just what was true and what wasn't. The whole affair was wholly unlike anything she had experienced in the past. She was really in love with Ralph, deeply in love with him. No other word but love could possibly convey the feeling she had for him.

But—

That, she admitted, was the hang-up. *But*. The almighty but, the omnipresent but, the little word that got in the way and turned everything upside-down.

But.

But me no buts, she thought fiercely. *But me no goddam buts.*

But where did she go from here?

It was as much of a mix-up as she could imagine, and thinking about it she had to laugh to herself. She was a lesbian, a dyed-in-the-wool, twenty-four karat, one hundred percent dyke, a man-hating, lady-loving daughter of Sappho—and she was in love with a man. It was so ridiculous it made her laugh and so horribly hopeless she felt like shooting herself.

And, to top it all off, she needed sex desperately. It had been quite a while now—a long time between drinks, and she was getting pretty damned thirsty. Not since Gloria, and that was how long? She couldn't stop to remember, but it was a long time.

She needed a woman.

It would be much nicer all around, she reflected, if she needed a man. Then she could go find Ralph and crawl in bed with him and they would both be happy. Then everything would be just hunky-dory, happy and all, and there would be no more problems for little Susan.

But it wasn't that way at all.

She needed a woman.

But who? What did you do when you needed a woman? She could do what she had always done—make the rounds of the gay bars until she ran into some other frustrated babe out on the town and hungry for a playmate. That was generally easy enough. Then off to somebody's bedroom and to hell with everything but the pure physical and emotional hunger that had drawn the two of them together in the first place.

But she didn't want that. That was the sort of thing she had never wanted, the blindly promiscuous craving that made most male and female homosexuals more than a little repulsive to her. It was as if their abnormality gave them a right to flout all the other conventions of the world along with the basic convention of heterosexuality. Once the one bridge was crossed, nothing was supposed to stand between them and the fulfillment of their physical needs.

She didn't go along with that notion. Just because she preferred women was no reason for her to take sex without anything more than unreasoning hunger. Why, there were men and women who chose sexual partners without so much as an interest in physical attraction! If those people just found somebody willing to sack out with them, that was all they were interested in. That wasn't her idea of the way to run your life at all.

Which left her right where she started from.

In love—but with no way to consummate that love. And in heat—with no way to cool off.

When the answer came to her she couldn't figure out how she had managed to go so long without thinking of it. It seemed tremendously obvious, and it was a wonder to her that it hadn't hit her mind right at the beginning.

Because there was a woman she was attracted to, a woman she had wanted from the moment she first laid eyes on her. A woman who wanted her and would be ready and willing to start an affair with her. A woman she wouldn't have to worry about hurting because the woman seemed to be immune to emotional pain.

A woman named Stella James.

Yes, it would be purely physical. And blindly promiscuous. All the things she reviled. But—

But Stella would want her; Stella would be quick to accept her love. And with Stella it could be quick and simple, a relationship based upon mutual need and mutual attraction, with no strings on either side. With Stella she wouldn't feel that she was cheating on Ralph, either—if only because the affair was going to be so basically empty on all but a physical plane.

Then she would be able to make up her mind. Once she unwound and was able to relax physically her mind would be able to work on the problem that was currently banging it into walls. Once she could lie down in Stella's arms for a quick and desperate orgasm, then the sex bit would leave her alone long enough for her to get some serious thinking done.

That was the answer.

She looked at herself in the mirror and decided quickly that a sloppy blouse and a pair of dungarees was hardly the outfit for a love affair. She changed into a dress—it was the first time in weeks she had had occasion to wear one. The dress was navy blue and it fit her figure perfectly, accentuating the calves and thighs and breasts. She went overboard and put on a pair of high-heeled shoes. She combed her hair very methodically until it was all quite perfect and placed a drop of her best perfume behind the lobe of each ear.

"You," she said to her reflection, "look remarkably young and lovely."

And she blew a kiss at the mirror and walked out of the apartment and down the stairs.

Now that her mind was made up she didn't waste time. She walked at once to the door of the first floor apartment and knocked three times. She wasn't even nervous anymore. Indecision was worse than any decision for her—once her mind was settled she was always much calmer, much more relaxed in every way. When Stella opened the door a smile came at once to her lips and stayed there.

Stella had spent the earlier part of the day doing next to nothing. She was dressed quite informally in comparison to Susan but looked lovely nevertheless. A skimpy polka dot halter encased her huge breasts and matching short-shorts covered her hips and thighs like a coat of paint. Her eyes lit up when she saw Susan.

"Well," she said. "Come in."

Wordlessly the girl followed her inside. Stella led the way to the couch in the front room and the two sat down on it side by side. Susan waited for Stella to speak; Stella, on the other hand, said nothing in an effort to force the younger girl to take the initiative.

Then Susan said, "I wanted to see you."

"Oh?"

Susan didn't say anything.

"Why?"

"I think you know why."

"To borrow a cup of sugar?"

"No."

"That's the general reason in the stories. People are always dropping in on other people to borrow a cup of sugar. I don't know—maybe the line's so worn out that nobody uses it anymore."

"I don't want any sugar."

"Oh?" A smile appeared on Stella's lips and light danced in her eyes. Susan's lips formed a thin line. She didn't smile. She didn't say anything.

"Well, you would have been out of luck if that's what you came for. I don't use sugar—don't even keep it around the house."

Susan was beginning to get annoyed. Making conversation was one thing but playing games was another. And she didn't want to play games.

For a moment she considered getting up and getting out. Hell, she wasn't so hard up that she had to chase after another woman. But she changed her mind and decided to stay. If Stella wanted to play it that way she would be willing to make the concession.

"If it wasn't sugar, what in the world did you come for?"

"You know."

"I do?"

"Of course you do."

"What makes you so sure?"

Susan's anger flared. "Damn it, you know what I came for and you want me. I know you want me—you made that obvious every time I've seen you. Why do you have to drive me crazy like this?"

Stella smiled.

"Please," Susan said. "Please."

"I'm sorry."

"Don't you want me?"

In answer Stella's hand dropped to Susan's thigh. The girl's flesh was soft but firm beneath the thin fabric of the blue dress. Stella's hand lingered there for a moment before she spoke, her fingers kneading the girl's thigh gently.

"Of course I want you."

"Then—"

"I just wanted to be sure," she went on. Her hand moved higher.

"How could you help being sure?"

Stella laughed. "You spend so much time with Ralph, I thought maybe I was wrong and you weren't gay after all. I guess I was mistaken."

Susan's mouth opened and she started to say how things were between her and Ralph, that she was in love with him. But the words refused to come out. Somehow she knew that this woman would only laugh at the private hell she was going through. She remembered what Ralph had said to her about Stella and decided that he was right.

Susan stood up. "If you want to talk," she said levelly, "you can find somebody else to talk to. I don't feel in the mood for conversation."

"Neither do I."

"Then—"

Stella stood up, the taunting smile fading into a stare of unashamed lust. "I want you," she said. "I've wanted you all along. Come here."

Susan moved closer to the woman. Their eyes met.

"Look at me."

Susan did as she was told. Slowly her eyes travelled the length of Stella's body, studying the swelling calves, the tightly muscled thighs, the wide hips and flat stomach and the high, full, glorious breasts. Her gaze took in the blonde hair, the perfect features, the deep eyes.

"Do you like what you see?"

Susan nodded. She couldn't speak.

"Take off my halter."

Her fingers trembling, Susan reached around the woman and groped for the catch on the polka dot halter. The movement brought their bodies together and Susan felt Stella's body press against her, felt the softness of her breasts and the strength in her hips and thighs.

After two false starts her fingers managed to undo the catch on the halter. She pulled it off and dropped it to the floor, her mouth forming a little O at the sight of Stella's breasts. They were so big, so perfect, so completely white except for the hard red nipples.

"Look at me."

The command was unnecessary. Susan couldn't have possibly looked elsewhere.

"Now the shorts."

Susan bent over and reached for the front of Stella's shorts. Her fingers had a great deal of trouble with the button at the top but she finally managed to get it open. Then came the zipper which was easier. When the zipper was unzipped she had to pull the shorts down over Stella's hips and thighs. The bigger girl stood completely motionless, making no move to assist her. At last the shorts dropped to the floor and Stella stepped out of them. All that remained was a pair of filmy white panties.

"The panties," Stella said. That was all she said, but Susan could tell that the woman was hungry and ready for her. She was breathing faster and harder now and her hand seemed to be shaking.

The panties were easy. Again Stella was completely motionless and again the girl had to do everything herself. When the brief panties rested on the floor Stella stepped out of them and kicked them across the room in one motion.

They stood completely still and wholly silent for almost a full minute. Susan felt strangely embarrassed, as if Stella was dressed and she herself the naked one instead of the other way around.

Then Stella said, "Now your clothes."

She took off her dress very precisely and methodically. For some reason there was no haste in the process—she wasn't in any rush at all. She was in the middle of something and she intended to go through with it. But that was all. Any hunger she had felt in the beginning, any lust for the other girl's beautiful body—it all had drained out of her for some reason which she couldn't begin to figure out.

She folded her dress neatly and placed it on the couch. Then she removed her bra and panties and put them, too, on the couch. She stood naked for a moment in her high-heeled shoes—then she took them off, too, and put them together at the foot of the couch.

Stella's eyes were bold. They stared at the hair she had taken so much time to comb and ran the length of Susan's body. They studied the small but perfect breasts a long time and then moved to the special place, the secret place, the place where no man had ever been. And for some incomprehensible reason Susan felt embarrassed and frightened, as if it were a man who was looking at her.

"You're very lovely, Susan."

"Thank you."

"Do you think I'm attractive?"

"You know you are."

"Tell me."

Pause.

"Tell me, Susan."

"You're . . . very beautiful."

"Thank you."

God, God, God. Why didn't they just do it and get it over with? Why all this preliminary nonsense that neither of them needed? Or perhaps this was what Ralph had meant when he talked of Stella's need to hurt, to dominate. Maybe her taunting had a purpose; maybe that was what Stella needed in order to enjoy what followed it.

Susan didn't know. All she knew was that she was beginning to regret the whole business. She wished vaguely that she was back in her own apartment by herself. But now that she was here she might as well get it over and done with.

"Give me your hand, Susan."

Stella took her by the hand and led her back to the bedroom. Susan went along without a word, accepting what was going to happen and walking with quick, nervous steps. The bedroom was messy and disordered, with the bed unmade and clothing scattered on the floor. The appearance of the room added a note of cheapness and illicitness to the whole affair and increased her apprehensions. Maybe it would have been better if she had just stayed by herself, alone and frustrated but at least safe—

"Lie down, Susan."

She sat down on the messy bed, then stretched out on it. She tried to close her eyes and relax but her eyelids refused to close and her body only grew more tense and rigid at the thought of relaxation. When she did manage to get her eyes shut her head began to reel and she felt as though she was going to be sick. She had to open her eyes once again in order to get her bearings.

"Wait here."

Susan waited; there was nothing else for her to do. Stella left the room for a moment and Susan tried to figure out where she was going or what she was going to do. Maybe she just wanted to keep her waiting, thinking that it would make her even more nervous than she already was. Well, if that was her idea, it was certainly working. A fine sweat broke out on Susan's forehead and she felt her palms growing moist with perspiration as well. She didn't want anything now except to be back in her own room, didn't want the sexual release that Stella was willing to provide her with, didn't want anything but peace and solitude and the safety of being alone.

For one wild minute she considered the idea of getting up and running out of the room, grabbing up her clothes and racing up the stairs and to hell with Stella James. But the moment passed and the thought went with it. She just didn't have the nerve to run away now.

After what seemed like much longer than it was, Stella strode back into the room. She didn't bother to explain where she had been or what she had been doing. Instead she sat down on the edge of the bed facing Susan. The familiar smile reappeared on her face.

She reached out a hand and stroked Susan's cheek. Susan tried to relax and respond to the touch but she found it impossible. She seemed to be frozen inside—Stella's hand on her cheek was nothing, just a lump of clay.

"You're lovely," Stella was saying, "and I want you very much. But I guess you know how much I want you."

Words of love. But this time they were just words, dead words, empty words. This time they meant nothing to her, meant even less than they must have meant to Stella. Instead of a sexual response Susan could think of nothing but the essential emptiness of the situation.

Stella's hand moved to her breast. Her hand was very large and her fingers encircled the breast, the nipple snug in the girl's palm.

The fingers began to manipulate the breast just as so many fingers had manipulated Susan's breasts so many times.

But this time it was nothing—no feelings whatsoever coursed through her body. There were times before when her sexual partner meant little or nothing to Susan, times when the woman involved was a good deal less attractive than Stella.

But never before had her body refused to respond.

Stella's thumb and forefinger found the nipple of Susan's breast and began to play with it. Stella pulled and squeezed at the nipple and it grew hard, but Susan knew that it was only a reflex. Fingering automatically made a nipple harden—and she was still unmoved, still unexcited, still cold and fully unresponding.

Stella smiled. "Don't you like what I'm doing?"

No answer.

"It's all right. I know you enjoy it—you'd just prefer to lie there while I do all the work. Well, that's all right, dear. I'm enjoying myself."

More caresses. More words.

Nothing.

Stella lowered her mouth to Susan's other breast and began to plant little kisses on the softness of it. Her tongue bathed the firm flesh and made little circles around the nipple. Her teeth found the nipple and tugged at it like a playful kitten with a ball of yarn, but the only sensation that hit Susan was one of pain mingled with irritation.

This was wrong—this wasn't what she had wanted at all. This was cheap, cheap and ugly and dirty inside. It wasn't love, but she hadn't wanted love. But it wasn't even good healthy animalism, wasn't even the strong and beautiful meeting of two bodies.

It was revoltingly tawdry, unexciting sex. It wasn't what she wanted, and all at once she knew what it was that she did want.

She wanted Ralph.

Ralph.

His face came into her mind—strong and masculine and, for the first time it seemed to her, attractive. The image brought a sensation of fear with it, but now for the first time the fear was tempered with something else. Ralph wouldn't hurt her—wouldn't do anything to her, not unless she let him, not unless she wanted him to. With Ralph whatever did happen would happen because both of them wanted it, because both of them needed it.

But this—

This was what she had known, what her entire sexual life had been. But it was no longer enough. She needed more.

Stella was still busy with her breasts, but it was as though it wasn't really happening, as though Stella's hands were the wind and Stella's mouth was the rain. They were nothing to her, nothing at all.

And, lying there on the bed, she felt like a prostitute. She felt lower than that—she felt like filth, cheap rotten filth that didn't have the guts to do what it wanted.

And she knew that she had to get away from Stella right away. Before it was too late.

She sat up suddenly on the bed, pushing Stella away from her as she did so. The woman's mouth went wide and the smile was gone from her face, replaced all at once by an expression of complete surprise.

"What's the matter?"

She couldn't talk.

"Damn you, what's the matter?"

Susan tried to stand up but Stella's arms held her where she was. She couldn't move. "Let go," she said. "Let go of me."

"Not until you tell me what's bugging you."

"Let go!"

Stella released her.

"I can't," Susan said. "I just can't go through with it and that's all there is to it."

"What are you talking about?"

"I can't . . . let you make love to me."

"Why not?"

"I just can't."

Stella's face clouded. "I don't get it," she said, honestly puzzled. "You were the one who came in here all hot to trot. What changed your mind?"

"I—"

"Wait a minute." Stella smiled again, sure of herself once more. "Haven't you ever done this before?"

It would be so easy to lie. So easy—

"Yes," she said. "I've done it before."

Sometimes lying wasn't as easy as it seemed.

"Then—"

"I just don't want to make love with you."

Stella took a deep breath. "Say that again."

She repeated it.

"You mean you're going to leave me like this—all steamed up with no place to go? Is that what you're trying to tell me?"

"I'm sorry—but that's it."

There was something new in Stella's eyes this time—something ugly and horrible. Her hands reached out and gripped Susan by the shoulders, her fingernails digging into the girl's flesh.

"That," she said, "is what you think."

"What do you mean?"

"I'm going to have you, sister. Even if I have to rape you in order to get you."

She twisted on the bed but she couldn't get away from Stella. The woman's hands held her tight and she wasn't strong enough to get away. Then Stella's body was coming down on hers, pinning her to the bed, and Stella's hands released her and encircled her back.

It was almost funny—she had been so afraid of men and here she was being raped by a woman!

Stella's mouth came down on hers and Stella's hips began to grind into hers. It would be easy to submit, easy to just lie there until Stella was done with her.

Easy.

But impossible.

Reaching out wildly, her hand fastened on a lamp on the dresser by the side of the bed. She yanked on it and pulled it free.

Then, swinging with all her might, she brought it down on the back of Stella's head.

CHAPTER 9

For a sickening moment Susan thought she had committed murder. Stella went limp all at once and collapsed upon her in a tired heap. Her breasts pressed against Susan's stomach and her head lay at a crazy angle on Susan's breast. She didn't seem to be breathing.

Susan felt for a pulse and found one. Then she noticed that the older woman was breathing, slowly and weakly but steadily. She waited for a moment to make sure that the breathing would continue; then she slipped out from under Stella's naked body and hurried into the front room.

She dressed quickly, not caring how she looked. She let herself out of the apartment and closed the door behind her, taking the stairs two at a time until she reached her own door. Once on the way her dress bunched up and she almost fell, but she managed to keep on going until she was back in her own room. She locked the door behind her and sat down heavily in the chair, barely able to breathe.

It was almost impossible for her to calm herself down. The full reality of what had taken place was just beginning to hit her head on and she didn't think she could take it. First she had been willing to offer herself to Stella. Then she didn't respond. Then she refused to participate, and finally the other woman was on the point of raping her, so wrapped up in what she was doing that it became necessary to knock her on the head and race out of the room like a frightened virgin running from a sex maniac.

Well, when you came right down to it, that's about what it had been—a frightened virgin running from a sex maniac. She herself was certainly a virgin, and there was no question about Stella's mental normalcy.

But for Christ's sake how had it all happened?

She stood up and walked to her door to make sure it was locked. For good measure she used the chain lock as well so that she would be able to see who was there before opening the door. But she was still tense, still tied up in knots inside. Relaxation was out of the question.

She picked up a magazine and leafed through it. It didn't interest her in the least. She took off her dress and hung it up in the closet, then took off her underclothes and put them in her laundry bag. She was physically clean but felt dirty and took two showers in a vain attempt to wash the taste of Stella James from her skin.

After the shower she got in bed and tried to follow the lead story in the magazine. She read the same page over and over and finally gave up. It was no use.

Instead she thought about Ralph. It was obvious to her that as long as she loved him she could never enjoy sex with anybody else. As this fact sank in she began to realize just how deep her attachment to him was. With the various women she had loved she had been faithful, but she still was able to respond to other girls even if she never indulged in an overt act of infidelity. But with Ralph the thought of sexual contact with anybody else became suddenly unthinkable. She had had dramatic proof downstairs, when a desirable woman had proved totally incapable of arousing her.

This was good, she thought.

Good—because it meant that her love for Ralph was a very genuine thing. And she wanted real love, love that could last.

But not entirely good. Because the thought of intercourse was still terrifying to her, still a thing that sent her into shivers. Maybe it was something she would get over, maybe she could learn to be normal, but—

Suddenly she had a tremendous desire to see the portrait Ralph was painting of her. Maybe just a peek—

She got out of bed and walked to the easel. It was covered with a cloth, and it would be very, very easy to lift the cloth and see what he had done. And it certainly wouldn't hurt anything; he would never find out and it wouldn't make any difference in the world.

No. No, when he wanted her to see it he would tell her. If he trusted her not to look at it, the least thing she could do would be to respect that trust. Firmly she forced herself to return to bed. She turned out the lights and snuggled beneath the sheet.

But it was hours before she finally fell asleep.

Ralph spent the next morning at the museum again. It was a good escape for him and one that he had used often in the first year or so in New York. But this morning he was just using it to kill time. It was better than a movie, and it was even cheaper. After a breakfast of eggs and coffee at a greasy spoon on Sixth Avenue he didn't have much money left.

He spent his last cent on lunch. That, he decided too late, was a hell of a stupid thing to do. It was a healthy walk back to the Village and the subway would have been infinitely more sensible. But the lunch—a plate of chili at a chili house on 47th Street that gave you a decent meal for well under a buck—was worth it.

And the walk, when you stopped to think about it, wasn't such a bad idea at all. It was another time killer, a good way to waste part of the afternoon before drifting up to see Susan for the next step in the disappointment routine. Hell, why bother to see her at all? He could walk east and then downtown and wind up on Skid Row and not have to worry about women anymore. All he'd worry about would be where he'd get the money for the next drink, and to hell with the world and Stella James and Susan Rivers.

And to hell with Ralph Lambert.

He pulled himself together and started walking south on Sixth Avenue. He walked slowly, not in any particular hurry to get any particular place. It was a nice day—sunny but not too hot, the humidity lower than usual for New York, the air relatively clean. Hell, it was a great day. But it would probably turn out to be a son of a bitch. They always did, time after goddamn time.

Sixth Avenue is a good street for a walk. At 42nd Street behind the public library is Bryant Park, with trees and benches and a drinking fountain. Then clear down to 14th Street the avenue is lined with small stores and restaurants and bars. It's a grand old street, with lots of places to look at and enough things going on to keep a person interested.

Then, from 14th Street on downtown is the Village, and no matter how much Ralph despised the Village some of the time it was never boring. He kept on walking, taking his time, stopping to watch workmen with steam shovels sweating to lay the foundation for a new office building, just a small Village office building for dentists and doctors but an office building nevertheless. He watched kids playing ball on 12th Street and he watched a pair of men making their way into one of the myriad of gay bars.

He took his time. He relaxed.

It was almost four o'clock by the time he reached Susan's apartment.

After he knocked she opened the door partway, then relaxed visibly when she saw that it was him. She undid the chain and opened the door the rest of the way and led him inside.

"You're a little late," she said.

"I was uptown. It took me awhile to walk back."

"Why didn't you take a train?"

He explained to her.

"That's ridiculous," she told him. "Why, you should have left yourself enough money for the subway. You could have taken the train straight home and I would have fixed you something to eat."

"It's all right. The exercise didn't hurt me."

"Exercise? A two-mile walk in this heat?"

"It's not that hot."

She shrugged. "Well, maybe it'll be cooler after I get my clothes off."

She undressed very quickly, very simply, not bothering to

leave the room while she did so. Right away he knew that it was going to be bad this time. He didn't feel toward her in the coldly impersonal, sexless way an artist is supposed to feel toward a model. He couldn't see her body simply as a work of art, simply as a body to be painted. He saw her as a woman he wanted, a woman he craved, a woman he needed more than he needed anything else in the world.

She sat down in the chair and assumed the standard pose at once—feet apart, face unsmiling, her hands covering her pubic area. Breathing slightly faster than usual he mixed paints on his palette and took his brush in his hand. He uncovered the canvas and looked at it; it was almost completed, almost finished. Just another session or two and he would be done.

Tentatively he touched the brush to the canvas. He painted very slowly, so tense that he knew he would only ruin the painting if he went any faster. He worked very carefully, very precisely.

After ten minutes he couldn't take it any longer. Every time he looked at her—her face, her legs, her breasts, the provocative position of her hands—his mind was on anything but painting. He felt himself getting weak in the knees and his hand was no longer at all steady. Once the brush slipped slightly and he cursed under his breath. He was able to rectify the slip with next to no trouble, but he was afraid the next one would be worse.

"Let's take a break," he suggested.

"I'm not tired."

He grinned. "I am."

She followed him into the kitchenette and they sat down together at the tiny kitchen table. He could feel the nearness of her, smell the clean fresh smell of her nakedness. He lit a cigarette and forced himself to look away from her, but his eyes came back to her in a second.

"Ralph—"

"What is it, darling?" The *darling* spilled from his lips automatically. If it bothered her she gave no indication of it.

"When can I see the picture?"

He considered. Probably there was no harm in showing it to her now. All that remained were a few strokes here and a few more there. And she had been patient enough for a hell of a long time.

"C'mon," he said. "You might as well have a look at it."

He took her by the hand and they walked back to the easel. Her hand was very small in his, very small and soft. He could smell the natural perfume of her body, could feel the softness of her as their bodies touched.

When she stood behind the easel with him, it was as though he himself was seeing the painting for the first time. Only then did he realize how good it was, how much better it was than anything he had ever done before. Every line had a purpose, every tone and shading was just right.

And it was her. That was the important thing, the thing that had to be right. It was her on the canvas, with every detail perfect from the smile on her face to the curves of her legs.

For a long time she didn't say a word. He still held her hand in his and she stood without moving, her eyes concentrating entirely on the picture.

Then, still without moving or turning her head, she asked, "Is that the way I look to you, Ralph?"

"Yes."

They were silent again. She still didn't move.

Then: "Honestly?"

"Honestly."

"I didn't realize I was that . . . beautiful."

"At least that beautiful. More beautiful, perhaps—but that's as good as I can do with paint on canvas."

She still did not avert her eyes from the canvas, and when she spoke it was in a soft monotone.

"I almost looked at it last night, Ralph. I wanted to."

"How come you didn't?"

"Because you told me not to."

"I would never have known."

She hesitated. "I'm glad I didn't," she said.

"How come?"

"This way we looked at it together. And it's nicer that way."

This time she moved. She turned her head toward him and there was a half-smile on her lips. He looked down into her eyes and all he could think of was how much he was in love with her, how much he wanted her, how desperately he needed her.

He put one arm around her. She didn't draw away from him.

He lowered his mouth to hers.

The kiss started off gentle and simple and still she didn't resist him. Then he started to draw her in closer so that her nude body pressed up against him. His tongue stroked her closed lips tenderly.

And, suddenly, she pulled away from him and hid her face in her hands.

•   •   •

"Susan!"

She walked away from him, shaking her head from side to side. He followed her and she sat down finally on the bed and made room for him to sit down next to her. After he did so he started to put an arm around her but she waved him away.

"Ralph," she said. "Darling, I have something to tell you and I want you to listen to me until I'm finished. All right?"

"Sure."

"I love you, Ralph."

He closed his eyes, sure that he knew what was coming. It would be the same song and dance they had gone through yesterday, the same I-love-you-but-nothing-can-come-of-it business she had spouted last afternoon.

"Go ahead."

"Please, Ralph—I don't want you to interrupt me at all. I'm not sure just how to word this and I don't want to louse it up."

When she paused he took his cigarettes from his shirt pocket and shook one loose. He put it between his lips and scratched a match, bringing the flame up to the cigarette. Her fingers touched his and she asked him for a cigarette without words, and he gave her one just as silently and lit it for her.

"Ralph, darling, every time I'm with you I love you a little more. And every time I'm with you and realize how much I love you, well, I begin to want you just that much more. But basically I'm still a very scared and frightened little kid."

He expelled a mouthful of smoke in a thin line and watched it break up into a shapeless cloud and drift lazily toward the ceiling.

"I'm afraid of a lot of things, Ralph. I'm afraid of you, for example."

One hand clenched into a fist. He could feel the tension in his jaw muscles, tried to relax and found it impossible. The fingers of his right hand tightened on the cigarette and he looked down helplessly as the slim cylinder of paper and tobacco was crushed between his fingers. Grains of tobacco spilled to the floor and he ground out the glowing tip of the cigarette with his heel.

"But, darling, every day I'm a little less afraid of you. Every day I relax more. I . . . I think I'm going to be able to get there, Ralph. I think I'm going to be able to love you . . . all the way."

He stared at her. For a moment he thought he had heard wrong.

"Yes, darling. This fear is a very strong thing, the biggest thing in my life so far. It's what drove me to women in the first place and it's the thing that has kept me from you so far. But I'm beginning to get over it. I knew this yesterday after you left and I'm beginning to know it more and more. Every minute I spend with you makes me more aware of how much you mean to me, how much I love you. Every time I—"

"Susan—"

"Let me finish, darling."

He stopped in mid-sentence.

"Every time I see you I can go a little bit farther, Ralph. But this fear of mine—it's a hell of a deep-seated thing. It's probably something so deep inside of me that the only way to find out the cause of it would be to see a psychiatrist, and even that would take years and might not work out after all. But I *think* it'll work out, if we give it time.

"You can't rush me, Ralph. If you rush me I'll just stay afraid and . . . and it won't do either of us any good. I love you tremendously but it's going to take time for us to work all this out and . . . and I want it to work out darling. I want it more than I ever wanted anything in the world."

They were both silent for several minutes. He turned slightly and saw that tears were beginning to form in the corners of her eyes, and very gently he said, "Of course it will work, Susan. Of course it will."

And then, without touching her or trying to kiss her, be talked to her. He told her how much he loved her, how much he needed her. He told her everything he had told her the day before and more because he loved her now far more than he had then, and because he knew now that he would love her more and more for the rest of their lives. He would never stop loving her, and he knew this, and he told her so.

Then, finally, he stood up.

"What's the matter?"

"I'd better go now."

"Why?"

"I'd just better leave."

"Don't you want to finish the picture?"

"Not now."

"Why not?"

"Light's not right."

"The light's still good."

He shrugged.

"Tell me, Ralph."

He hesitated. How in the world could he explain it to her?

"Ralph—"

He said, slowly: "Susan, men are . . . different from women. When you want somebody badly enough it gets into your blood and you . . . you can't think of anything else. Halfway things aren't enough. I mean—well, you have to make love or you can't think or concentrate or do much of anything."

Neither of them said anything. He stood there, fully clothed, and she sat naked on the bed. They looked at each other and it was minutes before either of them spoke a word.

Then she said, "Maybe I can help you, Ralph."

"What do you mean?"

She turned away from him. "Ralph, you've got to promise not to . . . do anything. I don't want you to touch me or kiss me or anything of the sort. Will you do that for me?"

"It'll be tough," he admitted.

"Will you promise?"

"I promise."

"Then take off your clothes."

He wasn't sure what was happening but he didn't want to argue. He unbuttoned his shirt and pulled it free from his trousers and slipped out of it. Then he took off his pants and put them with the shirt on a chair.

"All your clothes, Ralph."

He untied his shoelaces and took off his shoes and socks. Then he removed his underwear and stood before her completely naked.

"Now . . . lie down on the bed."

He did as he was told.

She sat down on the bed and leaned over him, her eyes probing deep into his. She smiled.

"See how much better I'm getting," she said. "This would have terrified me a day ago."

He smiled back at her.

"Remember," she said. "Don't touch me or say anything or kiss me. Don't . . . don't do anything at all."

He nodded.

Then she lowered herself to him and kissed him on the cheek. Her lips were soft and cool and she kissed him again, more firmly this time.

Her lips found his mouth and she kissed him a third time. It was all he could do to keep from wrapping his arms around her and kissing her hard, but somehow or other he managed to restrain himself. When her tongue slipped between his lips and tasted the inside of his mouth he wanted to return the kiss, to meet her tongue with his own. But he held himself back.

Her mouth moved to his throat. As she laid a string of little kisses up and down his neck her hands moved to his arms and her fingers kneaded his biceps muscles gently, tenderly. She kept kissing him, driving him out of his mind with hunger and love for her. He didn't think he could stand it any longer.

Her mouth moved lower and she began kissing him on the chest. Her tongue found his nipples and she kissed and licked each of them in turn, tugging on them almost as though he were a woman. He had trouble controlling his breathing and his heart was pounding like a pneumatic hammer.

"Ralph," she breathed. "I love you."

Her mouth moved lower. She bathed his stomach with her

warm tongue until his arms were rigid at his side with his fists clenched tighter than vises. He wanted to grab her, wanted to act on all the sexual passion that had been building up within him.

Her hands found his thighs and resumed the gentle kneading motion they had used on his upper arms. He writhed and twisted on the bed and began making small involuntary sounds in his throat. Her tongue flicked against the inside of his thigh like a snake and made him gasp for breath.

She didn't stop. She worked him into a frenzy, driving him wild with her lips and tongue until he was ready to scream for her to stop, to do anything but not to drive him insane this way.

Her tongue was busy again on the inside of his thighs. He raised his head to look at her, to say something to her, and as if on cue she looked up at him and stared into his eyes.

He returned her stare. In her eyes he saw all the love and passion and hunger in the world. Her lips parted and there was a deep, searching, penetrating stare in her eyes.

And at that instant he knew.

Maria ached.

That, she decided, was the only way to describe it. Why, she hurt all over! Her little bottom was all sore where Mummy spanked her and the rest of her body hurt in a million spots from the belt Mummy had used on her.

Maria hurt.

It wasn't fair, she decided. She had been bad, although she couldn't remember just what it was that had been so bad. But it didn't really matter. She was always being bad and her Mummy was always punishing her.

But did her Mummy have to hurt her so very much? It was really terrible. The spanking was bad enough, but it was nothing compared to the belt. The belt whooshing through the air, and she would lie there on the bed waiting for it and not knowing where it would hit, and then it would land and hurt her so terribly.

It just wasn't fair.

But she took her punishment like a good little girl. Yes, no matter how bad she was she would always take her punishment and be good about it. Why, sometimes she didn't even wait for her Mummy to call her but went straight in to her Mummy and told her that she had been bad.

Those times she was telling lies, of course. Why, there were times when she told her Mummy that she made mud pies just to make her Mummy mad so she would get her punishment. But that all evened it out, because by telling such bad lies she was being bad and deserved the punishment she got.

But Mummy was so mean—

The spankings were all right, she decided magnanimously. The spankings were okay, and even the whipping with the belt was all right even if it hurt so much she couldn't stand it.

But the burning—

That, she told herself firmly, was not right at all.

She fingered her breasts gingerly one at a time. Why, that wasn't right at all. That was a horribly nasty way to punish a girl. Now why in the world would Mummy do that, taking a cigarette and lighting it and holding the tip to each of Maria's nipples? Why, it was a perfectly horrid thing to do!

And it still hurt. Goodness knew how long it would hurt, because Mummy really held the cigarette there a long time and she only seemed to enjoy it even more when poor Maria squirmed and howled and tried to get away.

What a horrid thing to do!

That made Mummy a bad Mummy. But that didn't make any sense, because how could a Bad Little Girl have a Bad Mummy?

It didn't make any sense at all.

And she loved her Mummy.

But she also hated her Mummy.

It was all very confusing.

Chapter 10

Ralph lay on his side on the bed. Susan was snuggled up close to him, the top of her head just level with his lips. Without moving he kissed her gently and smiled when she murmured something that he didn't hear.

He was at peace, completely and totally at rest. It was a peace he had never known before, a compelling and overwhelming peace that left him entirely drained of everything but a monumental love for her.

They were both naked, both wrapped up in each other's arms. He held her as if he were holding some rare and delicate bird that would die if he held it too tight. Her body was soft and warm against him.

"I love you," he said.

She murmured again.

"You're the most wonderful thing that ever happened to me, Susan. You're . . . you're wonderful—that's all I can say."

She didn't answer.

"Susan . . . Susan, I want you to marry me. You will marry me, won't you, baby?"

Slowly she raised herself up on one elbow and looked at him with eyes that were brimming over with love.

"Are you sure you want me to?"

"Of course I'm sure."

"Marriage is a pretty big thing."

"Marriage is forever," he said. "To me marriage is something that has to be forever."

"Forever is a long time."

"I know it."

"Are you sure you'll want me . . . forever?"

"Positive."

She pressed her lips to his throat and kissed him, a long, soothing kiss that had no passion to it but an infinite amount of love.

"If you want me," she said, "I want you."

He took her face in his hands and kissed her all over it—her eyes, her nose, her ears, her lips and her chin, little sexless kisses all over her face. She smiled up at him.

"I want to stay here tonight," he said.

"All right."

"Aren't you . . . afraid of me?"

"What do you mean?"

"If I'm here all night, there's no telling what I might do."

"I'm not afraid."

"Are you sure?"

"Of course, Ralph. I don't think I could ever be afraid of you."

He kissed her. Then they snuggled up close again and she reached up and turned out the light. It was still quite early and they lay together for hours, whispering and touching each other, kissing like schoolchildren and talking about what they would do and where they would live when they were married.

They were both fully relaxed. Neither had to do anything to prove that they were in love, and they rested together as two people can rest only after lovemaking that is completely satisfactory to both parties, lovemaking that is a part of love.

And, hours later, they fell asleep. They slept all night in one position with their bodies close together and their arms around each other.

The wind made noises outside the window. Once, in the middle of the night, the wind managed to blow up a storm with thunder and lightning. The rain poured down for almost an hour and the lightning ignited the sky and the thunder cracked and rumbled.

They never noticed it. They were in love and they were asleep, asleep with each other, and the rain and the thunder and the lightning might just as well never have happened.

Ralph woke up first. The first thing he was aware of, even before he remembered where he was and who he was and that it was morning, was the woman he held in his arms. He tried to get out of bed without waking her, but as soon as he made the first movement her eyes came open and she smiled at him.

"Good morning," she said.

"Good morning."

"Did I ever tell you I'm in love with you?"

"Dozens of times."

"Honest?"

"Sure enough."

"Well," she said, sleepily, "I was telling the absolute truth."

"Good thing you were."

"Mmmmmmm."

He smiled to himself and kissed her eyes shut. "Go back to sleep," he told her. "I'll be back in a little while."

"Where are you going?"

"Out."

"That's a hell of an answer."

"You want a better answer?"

"Mmmmmmm."

"I'm going to the bank," he said. "I've got about a hundred bucks in an account in my name and I want to draw it out."

"What for?"

"For us to get married on."

She thought for a minute. "You know," she said, "I couldn't possibly think of a better use for the money. As a matter of fact, I couldn't possibly think of a better reason for you to sneak out of bed and leave me alone."

"It's a good reason."

"A hell of a good reason," she said. "But hurry back."

He kissed her and pulled himself out of bed.

He dressed but his clothes were dirty and he stopped downstairs to change them. He made as little noise as possible inside his own apartment in an effort to avoid waking Stella. He changed quickly into a white sport shirt and a pair of cord slacks and left the apartment as quietly as he had entered it.

But he woke Stella.

Stella didn't move until Ralph was gone from the apartment. She didn't want to see him any more than he wanted to see her, as it happened. But the moment the door closed and he was gone, she clambered out of bed and put on her clothes, the same polka dot shorts-and-halter set she had been wearing the day before.

She washed and brushed her teeth in a hurry, but didn't bother about breakfast. There was something she had to do, something that had to be done in a hurry. There was no way to tell how much time she had left.

She put her hand on the back of her head and cursed softly to herself. Susan Rivers swung a mean lamp—there was no question about it. Her head still ached and there was a lump where the blow had landed. She cursed again and sat down for a moment on the couch, thinking.

There was something she had to do. It had to be done and it had to be done in a hurry. Part of her knew that it was something she shouldn't do, something she should go back to bed and forget about.

But she couldn't.

No, she had to go through with it. No matter how it turned out, no matter what happened to her, she couldn't get the notion out of her head. Last night she had tried desperately to take out all of her aggressions on Maria, but all she succeeded in doing was reducing the poor little thing to a mass of quivering, aching flesh. Her own hungers remained unabated; her own lusts stayed just as strong as they had been to begin with.

And so she had to do the Thing. It was a Thing with a capital T by now, because it had grown to assume rather immense proportions in her mind.

The Thing had to be done.

She slipped a pair of sandals onto her feet and walked to the door of the apartment. She opened the door, looked around, walked through it and closed the door behind her. The hallway was empty, the building happily quiet. She walked to the stairway and began mounting the stairs, anxious to do the Thing.

The Thing was very simple.

She was going to rape and murder Susan Rivers.

Susan was still dozing when the knock came on her door. If she had been fully awake things might have been different. Then she would have thought clearly, and if she'd thought clearly she would possibly have refused to open the door. At least she would have asked first who it was.

But, as it happened, she was not fully awake. And it didn't even enter her mind that the person knocking at the door could be Stella James. For that matter, she didn't even stop to think that the person knocking at her door could be anyone else in the world but Ralph.

And she wanted to see Ralph.

She pushed the covers back and slipped out of bed. Because she assumed that it was Ralph at the door she didn't even take the trouble to slip into a robe. Ralph was used to seeing her naked, and certainly there was no point in dressing up now for him.

She padded across the floor to the door. Some reflex made her hesitate for the briefest second with her hand on the doorknob, but the reflex wasn't enough to keep her from opening the door for Ralph.

Except, of course, that it wasn't Ralph at the door. Not at all.

It was a woman—a tall blonde dressed in a polka dot halter, polka dot shorts, and a pair of sandals.

It was, naturally, Stella James.

Susan didn't entirely believe her eyes for a second. But, automatically, she took a quick step backwards.

And this was fortunate; because if she hadn't done this Stella's hands would have encircled her neck. As it was Stella lunged forward with her hands outstretched and missed and Susan managed to jump back again and out of the way.

But Stella was inside the door now. And the insane light in the woman's eyes made Susan want to shriek her lungs out for help.

Now she was awake. Now she was wide awake, wide awake and thoroughly terrified and moving away from Stella into the kitchenette, just trying to get away, trying to put as much distance between the two of them as possible.

She wanted to scream. Oh, God how she wanted to scream. But how did you go about screaming early in the morning? Her mouth opened wide but no sounds came out of it. She tried desperately to launch a scream but only a strangled sob tore forth from her throat.

Stella came closer.

Susan couldn't run any further. Her back was to the wall of the kitchenette, with cupboards and drawers on one side of her and the sink on the other.

There was, suddenly, no place to go, no way to turn, no one to help her. She wished that Ralph was there.

She might as well have wished for wings.

Again she tried to scream and again she was too petrified to launch the cry. Instead she said, her voice little more than a whisper, "What . . . what do you want?"

"You."

"What—"

Stella spaced her words very carefully and enunciated with the utmost precision, and while she talked she stopped moving closer to Susan.

"You led me on," she said. "You led me on and got me all excited and then you left me. That wasn't the right thing for you to do. It was wrong, and it is my duty to punish you."

"Look, you've got to understand! It was all a mistake, I didn't mean—"

"You've got to be punished," Stella said. "First I'm going to have you as I wanted to do yesterday. And then I am going to punish you."

"Please—"

"Don't beg," Stella said.

Susan realized that she was dealing with a madwoman, that nothing she could say or do would change Stella's mind for her. And Susan had a fairly good idea of what Stella's concept of punishment would turn out to be.

Stella was going to kill her.

She didn't want to die. Suddenly she realized just how much she didn't want to die, just how much she had to live for. All at once the beauty of the life she and Ralph were going to have together hit her full force and the thought of losing all that was too much to bear.

I've got to stop her, she thought desperately. I've got to find some way to stop her.

She didn't try to scream anymore. Now that she understood what was happening she realized that a scream would probably provoke Stella to immediate action and cost her her life as a result.

Stella took another step toward her.

"Wait!"

Stella paused.

And then Susan realized something very important. As long as she managed to keep the older woman talking she was all right. As long as she kept the conversation going, no matter how insane the conversation became, Stella wouldn't attack her.

"Tell me," she said. "Why do you want me?"

"Because I hate you." Stella made the words convey the feeling that people only wanted those they hated. The thought alone chilled Susan.

"You hate me?"

"Of course."

"Why?"

"You must know why."

"But I don't know why, Stella. Please tell me."

The older woman shrugged impatiently. She took another step forward, her eyes blazing. Susan had to say something, had to say something in a hurry. As long as she kept talking, as long as she went on with conversation, any sort of conversation, then—

"Is it because of Ralph?"

"What about Ralph?" Stella seemed interested and Susan pursued the topic.

"Ralph and I are in love. Is that why you hate me?"

"What are you talking about?"

"Ralph and I are in love," she said again. "We're going to be married."

"You're lying to me."

"No, Stella. It's the truth. So help me God it's the truth."

"You're lying to me."

"Stella, it's the truth!"

"Tell me about it," Stella said. "Tell me all about you and Ralph."

Susan began talking furiously, talking about how she and Ralph had met that first morning, how they went to breakfast together, how he had painted her portrait and how in the interim they fell in love. She told Stella things she didn't think she would ever tell anybody in her whole life—how she loved Ralph but was afraid of him at the same time, how he loved her, how she tried to save herself from sexual frustration by a visit to Stella's room, how Ralph had come to her just yesterday and how they slept all night with their arms around each other. She talked as quickly as she could, embellishing everything with a wealth of detail, telling the older woman what they were wearing and what they said and on and on and on, spilling out all the details in an effort to keep Stella's mind off the murder she was about to commit.

She talked a mile a minute but her mind traveled elsewhere while she talked. It wasn't necessary for her to concentrate on what she was saying. Everything she said was something that had penetrated so deeply into her own brain that she could rattle it off without even thinking about it.

Her mind was busy with other things. Her mind had to figure

out a way for her to escape from Stella once and for all. After a while either she would run out of words or Stella would run out of interest and it would be all over. And she knew that she was no match for Stella in a fight. The big woman was much stronger than she was, and only a lucky accident had enabled her to knock Stella unconscious the day before.

She would need luck now.

Luck, and more than luck. Luck and a plan, luck and a way out of it all.

She needed something. Oh, Christ, if only she had listened to Gloria and bought a gun. It would have been easy enough for her to get a permit, and having a gun around the house would be nice just about now.

It was funny—Gloria advised her to get the gun to protect herself from men. But that was when she worried about men, and now she needed a weapon of some sort to protect herself from a woman! A lesbian's greatest fear traditionally was getting raped by a man—and now her own greatest worry was getting raped and murdered by a woman.

If only she had a gun. But she didn't have a gun, and she was going to need something in a hurry. She kept on talking full speed but she could see that Stella's attention was wandering. The woman was getting impatient. It was only a question of time, only a minute or two before Stella came at her with one desperate lunge and—

A knife.

That might do it. Maybe if she could get a knife from the drawer next to her. But would she be able to do it before Stella realized what she was doing? She had the feeling that if she so much as turned her eyes away from the other woman's eyes, Stella would make her move.

But she had to do something. And she was running out of things to do.

Her eyes still staring into Stella's eyes, Susan reached to her right. Her hand fumbled around and found the handle of the kitchen drawer. Oh, God, it had to be the right drawer!

She kept talking. Then, using her right hand only, she began to pull the drawer open a half-inch at a time. It stuck at first as it had a habit of doing and she almost died inside, but she gave another little tug and it came open.

Bit by bit she pulled on the drawer. When it was open almost four inches she let her hand slip inside, fumbling helplessly around for a knife. Accidentally she started to pick up the little paring knife and gripped it by the blade, wincing as the cold steel bit into her hand.

But it was just a nick, just a little cut. She held Stella's eyes with her own and groped around in the drawer until her fingers fastened around the heavy wooden handle of the breadknife.

The breadknife. Five inches of strong sharp steel. That would do it if anything would. That would save her.

And just as she gripped onto the breadknife she ran out of things to say to Stella.

There was a period of silence that was all of ten seconds long but that seemed to last forever. Stella's eyes bored into hers and her fingers tightened around the handle of the knife until she thought the wood would split between her fingers. She wanted to lift the knife out of the drawer but she was afraid, afraid that she would attract Stella's attention to what she was doing before she could get the knife ready for action. How long would it take? The knife was bulky and the drawer was open only a little ways, and her whole body seemed numb with fear. How quickly would she be able to react? How quickly would Stella move?

She didn't know. She couldn't take any chances, not until she absolutely had to, not until there was no choice anymore.

Stella said, "The painting."

For a moment she didn't realize what the woman was talking about. Then it came to her and she waited for Stella to go on.

"The painting. He painted a picture of you."

"Yes," she said desperately. "That's right, Stella. Ralph painted a picture of me."

"He painted one of me once."

"I know. He told me."

"The one of me was very beautiful."

"I'm sure it was."

"Very beautiful."

"You're a very beautiful woman," Susan said.

Stella smiled.

"I want to see the picture," Stella said.

"Oh—it isn't finished yet."

"Show it to me."

Susan took a deep breath. "It's over there," she said, nodding her head in the direction of the easel. When Stella turned to look toward the easel, the girl lifted the knife easily from the drawer and held it at her side. It seemed so easy, so simple.

When Stella turned back to Susan again she was looking directly at the knife.

She smiled. And Susan felt her stomach turning over. The woman was mad, raving, hysterically mad.

"You're a bad girl," Stella said. "You shouldn't play with knives."

"Get out of here or I'll kill you."

"You'd better give me the knife," Stella suggested. "You'd better give me the knife and stop being such a bad little girl."

"Stella!"

The woman took a step closer. Susan could reach her now with the knife. All she would have to do was stab out blindly, stab the knife into Stella's stomach and it would all be over. Then she would be safe.

"I'll kill you," she warned. "Do you hear me, Stella?"

Stella smiled again. She took another little step, her right hand reaching out for the knife.

Susan tried. With all her strength she tried to lift the knife and drive it home into Stella's belly. But something just went wrong somewhere and she couldn't quite manage it. She couldn't seem to move at all.

Lazily, easily, Stella's hand moved and took the knife from the girl's numb fingers.

It was all over now, all over for her. She knew that, and she stood very still with her eyes on the knife that was now in Stella's hand, the tip of the blade pointing toward her heart. In another second or so it would be all over forever, and she would never see Ralph again, never feel safe and secure in his arms again, never love him and be loved by him again.

She wanted to cry but she couldn't cry any more than she could scream or stab. She was numb and frightened, and her heart was beating so fast and her breath coming so quickly that she thought she was going to pass out cold. Well, she might as well faint. She would be just as dead in a moment anyway.

Stella smiled again, the sick smile, the twisted smile, the maniacal smile.

"The picture," she said. "I want to see the picture."

She walked all alone to the easel, the knife still in her hand, the insane smile still fixed on her face. She ripped the cloth covering off and stared down at the canvas while Susan cowered against the wall in the kitchenette, too petrified to move.

"The picture is very beautiful," Stella said.

Susan barely heard her.

"Very beautiful," Stella repeated. "Too beautiful to live. Too beautiful to go on living."

Susan was shaking uncontrollably.

"I'm going to kill you," Stella said.

Susan wanted to shout at her to go ahead and get it all over with. But something made her stop. And suddenly she realized that the woman was no longer paying any attention to her. Stella's mind was on the picture, and all her interest was focused upon it.

"I'm going to kill you," she repeated. "Kill you because you're too beautiful to live."

But she wasn't talking to Susan any longer. She was talking to the picture.

She raised the knife. Savagely she slashed away at the canvas. The first stroke of the knife went through Susan's portrait diagonally, slicing through the left breast and the right side of the stomach.

The next stroke was a stab wound where the heart would have been in the painting. Then another slash across the groin.

Stella kept on wielding the knife, making ribbons out of the canvas. Finally she was through and the knife dropped to the floor with a clatter. She turned from the portrait and walked back to where Susan was huddled against the wall in the kitchenette.

"You're dead," she said calmly. "I killed you."

Susan thought hysterically, *Ralph's going to be upset when he sees what she did to the picture.*

"You're dead," Stella repeated. "Why don't you fall down if you're dead?"

Susan crumpled up, exhausted, and dropped to the floor.

CHAPTER 11

Stella hurried downstairs. As she passed the second floor landing she shouted Maria's name. Somehow it seemed very important for her to see Maria just now. She wasn't sure exactly why, but she wanted very much to see Maria.

She didn't wait for the girl. She continued on downstairs the same smile still on her lips, the same insane light in her eyes.

She felt wonderful.

The strange thing was that she wasn't quite sure what had happened upstairs. She knew that she had killed somebody but it was difficult to determine just who it was that she killed. A girl, certainly. Yes, she remembered quite clearly that she killed a girl.

But who was the girl?

A knife. Yes, she could remember a knife. She took a knife and cut the girl in the breasts and the stomach and the groin and the legs and the throat. She cut the girl all over.

But who was the girl?

Susan Rivers. Yes, that was it of course. That was who it was. She remembered quite clearly now that she killed Susan Rivers. But which Susan Rivers?

Were there two Susan Rivers—one that moved and one that sat in a chair? That was possible, but how could that be? Maybe they were twins. But if they were twins, how come they both had the same first name? Twins were supposed to have different first names, weren't they?

Oh, it was all too much for her to try to figure it out. The hell with it. All that she knew for sure was that she had killed a girl and now she felt much better.

And Maria was coming, and that was good also. For some reason she wanted very much to see Maria.

She walked into her own bedroom and sat down on the edge of the bed with her back to the door. She reached around behind her and undid her halter, letting it fall to the floor. There—that was much better. It gave her breasts room to breathe, and it was very important for her breasts to have room to breathe.

Then she kicked off her sandals. Then finally she slipped out of her shorts and dropped them on the floor with the halter and the sandals.

To hell with it. Let everything stay on the floor. She wanted her little girl. Her Maria.

There were footsteps in the hallway, then footsteps in the front room. That was probably Maria, she thought. That was Maria, her little daughter, and Maria was coming to take care of her.

She didn't turn around.

The footstep came closer. Yes, that was Maria. She could recognize Maria's footsteps, and now Maria was coming into the bedroom.

"Hello," she said. "Hello, Maria."

But Maria didn't answer. That wasn't very good of Maria, and now she would have to punish the girl. It was all very tiresome but there was nothing else to be done. Maria was being bad and now she would have to be punished. She would have to learn to behave, and it was up to her Mummy to teach her what was right and what was wrong. Why, if her Mummy didn't teach her, how in the world would the bad little girl ever learn to be good?

There was a slight whirring sound in the air behind her and Stella started to turn around.

She didn't make it.

The heavy base of the lamp caught her on the skull just an inch or so away from the spot where Susan had struck her the other afternoon.

And, for the second time in as many days, Stella was knocked unconscious.

Maria worked very quickly and economically.

First she took a bedsheet from the linen closet and cut it into strips with a straight razor she found in the medicine chest. She laid Stella down on her back on the bed and used four of the strips to tie her hands and feet to the four posts of the bed.

She took another strip and placed it in Stella's mouth, tying it around the back of her head so that it would act as a gag and prevent Stella from making any sounds whatsoever.

She was very thorough. All of the five strips were tied very securely. The knots were quite tight and it would be impossible for Stella to move at all.

Then Maria sat down on the edge of the bed and waited for Stella to wake up.

Stella was not unconscious long. After what seemed to Maria like just a minute or two she opened her eyes and stared up at Maria.

Maria stared back. Then she started to giggle, because her Mummy looked very silly all tied up like that. Now she couldn't punish Maria anymore. She couldn't hurt her with the palm of her hand or the belt or the cigarette.

Not anymore.

Stella tried to say something, but Maria couldn't figure out for the life of her what it was her Mummy was trying to say. The gag stopped her from saying anything at all, and that was funny too.

Maria giggled again.

"Hello," she said. "Hi, Mummy."

Stella didn't answer, which was natural enough when you come right down to it.

"I was a bad girl, Mummy," she said. "I was a very bad girl. I got my clothes dirty playing in the sandbox and I said sassy things to my teacher and I broke Billy Rumsey's shovel. Wasn't I bad, Mummy?"

She giggled again. Oh, this was fun! Why, she was having a marvelous time.

"Mummy? Are you going to punish me, Mummy?"

Silence. Why, how nice it was of Mummy not to interrupt her. But Mummy wasn't answering her questions, and that wasn't especially nice. Why, it wasn't even polite, and Mummy always told her how important it was to be polite and answer when somebody asked you a question.

Maria let her hands wander over Stella's body. Mummy certainly had a lovely figure, that was for sure. Her breasts were especially nice, and Maria stroked and caressed and kissed her breasts over and over, hoping that her Mummy would enjoy what she was doing to her and what she was going to do. She took the nipples of Stella's breasts in her mouth one at a time and sucked them like a little baby girl until they grew hard and rigid.

Maria giggled.

"Mummy," she said softly.

Silence.

"I hate you, Mummy."

Why, what a horrid thing for her to say. That wasn't nice at all, and now Mummy would punish her for saying that. She was supposed to love her Mummy, wasn't she?

"I hate you, Mummy."

Now why did she have to go and say it again? It wasn't nice at all, and she certainly didn't want Mummy to punish her again. Mummy punished so hard and hurt her so much.

"Mummy," she said a third time, "I hate you."

And she giggled again.

Then she picked up the straight razor. She opened it and held it up to the light so that she could see it very clearly. The metal reflected the light and was very shiny, and the edge was very sharp.

Maria bent over again and kissed each of her Mummy's nipples in turn.

And then she cut each of them off with the razor.

Ralph sensed something was wrong the minute he saw Susan's door open. He rushed into the room. She was lying on the floor naked, her chest heaving and a cold sweat covering her forehead. He knelt down beside her and took her in his arms and she grabbed him as if she were drowning.

"Darling! What's the matter?"

For a few moments she couldn't answer. All she could do was remain in his arms and tell him how much she loved him. He held onto her and stroked her like a little kitten until finally her breathing went down to normal and she could speak again.

Then she told him.

She told him first how she had gone to see Stella the afternoon before. She told him the whole scene that had taken place between the two of them, with Stella trying to make love to her and attempting at last to rape her until she finally knocked her out and escaped.

Then he interrupted her.

"Baby," he said, "why didn't you tell me this before?"

"I don't know."

"I mean—"

"I suppose I was a little bit ashamed of myself, Ralph."

"That's ridiculous."

"I guess so."

"You don't have to be ashamed of anything, darling."

She kissed him and continued, telling him this time about the scene with Stella that had just taken place. His eyes went wide as she recounted what the woman had done, and several times he was at the point of interrupting her, but he let her finish.

"I knew she was sick," he said slowly after she had finished.

"Very sick, Ralph."

"Sicker than I realized. My God, she almost killed you!"

She nodded.

"What an awful woman," he said. "To think I was actually living with her."

"The painting's completely ruined, Ralph."

"To hell with the painting."

"But—"

"I could paint it again blindfolded. It's you that I'm worried about. She might try something like that again and there won't be a painting for her to slash up by mistake."

"I don't know she will. She thinks she killed me."

He shook his head. "I better call the police," he said. "She ought to be put away."

He started to stand up.

"Wait, Ralph."

He turned and looked at her.

"The police can wait."

"But—"

"Let them wait, darling. There's something I want you to do for me first."

"Anything."

She stood up and came into his arms. She was still trembling slightly, but her trembling was not from fear this time.

"I want you to make love to me, Ralph. All the way."

He took off his clothes again and put them on the chair. When he was naked and ready for her she was already lying on the bed. He lay down beside her and took her in his arms, kissing her.

She was not afraid.

He kissed and stroked every square inch of her body. He touched her and kissed her and caressed her until she turned into a woman on fire with love, a thing of passion writhing on the bed beside him.

She was not afraid.

And then he took her. He took her slowly, gently, and at first it hurt but a second later she didn't notice the pain at all because it was all so good and so beautiful, all so perfect and so wonderful, all so absolutely excellent and so unlike the way she had imagined it.

Their bodies moved together. She was on a gigantic seesaw going up and down, up and down, up and down, and she thought that it would never end because it kept getting better and better and she was going wild, wild, and it was so good, so unbelievably good.

And then it was over. Their bodies melted apart and she knew a peace that she hadn't believed existed. She laughed and then she cried and then they were both very still.

He looked at her and she knew the question he wanted to ask.

She said, "It was the most beautiful thing that ever happened to me."

And it was.

They were silent.

And then she said, "Ralph?"

"What is it, darling?"

"Could you . . . I feel like a wanton."

"What is it?"

"Could you . . . make it happen again?"

When the police came to the first-floor apartment at 69 Barrow Street they found a little brunette sitting on the floor in the bedroom with a razor in her hand. She was giggling hysterically to herself and mumbling baby talk.

What they found on the bed caused one of them to be thoroughly sick in the bathroom.

Another group of men came and took Maria to the hospital for the criminally insane. She became very well known there as the little girl who stole a bottle of rubbing alcohol from the dispensary and poured it into her vagina as penance for what she had done to her Mummy.

Still another crew of men shoveled what was left of Stella into a box. They took the box to the morgue and it stayed there for a few days. Then some other men took it away and buried it.

Ralph and Susan didn't remain at 69 Barrow Street. Too many things had happened there that both of them wanted to forget. Besides, the Village represented a way of life that each of them had no desire to stick with.

They moved to an apartment on 94th Street near Riverside Drive. It wasn't long before Ralph landed a good job doing covers for a paperback book outfit. It wasn't too much longer before they had their first child, a boy.

But the Village remained and it will remain forever. Stella and Maria and Ralph and Susan have left it, but the other Sick Ones will be there forever. Luke and Betty Swinnerton will stick needles of heroin into their arms until they pop their way to hell. The others will smoke marijuana and drink too much and sleep with whoever asks them until they rot and die.

The Village endures.

My Newsletter: I get out an email newsletter at unpredictable intervals, but rarely more often than every other week. I'll be happy to add you to the distribution list. A blank email to lawbloc@gmail.com with "newsletter" in the subject line will get you on the list, and a click of the "Unsubscribe" link will get you off it, should you ultimately decide you're happier without it.

Lawrence Block has been writing award-winning mystery and suspense fiction for half a century. You can read his thoughts about crime fiction and crime writers in *The Crime of Our Lives*, where this MWA Grand Master tells it straight. His most recent novels are *The Girl With the Deep Blue Eyes*; *The Burglar Who Counted the Spoons*, featuring Bernie Rhodenbarr; *Hit Me,* featuring Keller; and *A Drop of the Hard Stuff,* featuring Matthew Scudder, played by Liam Neeson in the film *A Walk Among the Tombstones.* Several of his other books have been filmed, although not terribly well. He's well known for his books for writers, including the classic *Telling Lies for Fun & Profit,* and *The Liar's Bible.* In addition to prose works, he has written episodic television (*Tilt!*) and the Wong Kar-wai film, *My Blueberry Nights.* He is a modest and humble fellow, although you would never guess as much from this biographical note.

Email: lawbloc@gmail.com
Twitter: @LawrenceBlock
Facebook: lawrence.block
Website: lawrenceblock.com